DESPERATELY SEEKING SUSPECTS

Books by D.A. Wilkerson

Totally 80s Mysteries

A Totally Killer Wedding
Most Likely to Kill
Of Heist and Men
A Totally 80s Christmas
Desperately Seeking Suspects

Mystery Journals

Mysterious Musings
My Totally Suspect Notebook

Books by Dana Wilkerson

Throwback RomComs

More Than Pen Pals
So Much More
Truth or More Truth

DESPERATELY SEEKING SUSPECTS

Totally 80s Mysteries Book 5

D.A. WILKERSON

D.A. Wilkerson
Mystery Author
danawilkerson.com

Desperately Seeking Suspects

Totally 80s Mysteries Book 5

by D.A. Wilkerson

© 2025 Dana Wilkerson

Designed in the USA

Images and fonts used under license by Canva

Published by Dana Wilkerson, LLC

Edmond, OK

danawilkerson.com

First Edition: June 2025

Paperback ISBN: 978-1-948148-38-2

eBook ISBN: 978-1-948148-39-9

Dedicated to all the small town residents who are relieved a murder doesn't take place in their town every few months

Chapter One

February 1986

"The countdown's on," my best friend Trixie said as I slid into our usual booth at The Checkered Cloth—locally known as The Check—our favorite diner in downtown Cherry Hill. "You have about a week until Mitchell and Marty expect you to tell them if you're going to date either of them. What are you going to do?"

I groaned and dropped my head into my hands. I'd been putting off my decision for nearly two months now. "It's too early in the morning for me to think about that."

It was 6:30 on Thursday morning, which was well before my usual wake-up time, since I didn't need to be at my secretarial job across the street at First Community Church until 8:30. But Trixie's husband Scott gave her a Christmas present that also typically included me. He told her he'd get their kids ready and take them to school two days a week, so she could do whatever she wanted during that time.

Sometimes she went to her high school math classroom early

to get some work done, and one time she tried—and failed—to sleep in, but usually she wanted to meet me for breakfast at The Check. The two of us spent a lot of time together, but the kids were almost always around. I loved Krystal and Victor as if they were my own niece and nephew, but I also enjoyed adults-only time with my best friend, which was why I agreed to roll out of bed early whenever she asked.

Trixie tapped her fingernails on the table. "Well, you're going to have to tell them something, even if it's that you still don't know. You have to put Marty out of his misery. That man has been moping around town ever since Christmas, and it's not only because he got knocked over the head with a baseball bat."

My heart squeezed at the thought that my actions might be hurting Marty. He was such a good man.

"He's really moping?" I had done my best to avoid him since he told me he loved me and I told him I needed space to figure out what I wanted for my future.

Trixie shrugged. "Not all the time, but you don't like the thought that he might be, do you?"

I shook my head. "No. I hate that I've already caused him so much pain."

"I know that, but it wasn't your fault. You didn't know how he felt."

"But I should have." I took a big bite of my blueberry pancakes as I slumped down in my seat.

"No, you shouldn't have. You were dating another man."

"But Marty didn't know that." I dated Detective Mitchell Crowe secretly for months before discovering my friend Marty James had feelings for me.

"Yeah," Trixie said as she pointed a forkful of scrambled eggs at me, "you probably shouldn't have left him in the dark about that, but there's nothing you can do about it now. And Marty could've let you know about his feelings much earlier. But what's done is done, and you need to stop procrastinating and figure out if you want to be with either of those guys. You're lucky they both care enough about you that they'd give you two months to decide what you want for your future, but here we are in mid-February, and you don't seem to know what you want now any more than you did then."

I really didn't, and it wasn't for lack of thinking about it. The two men were so different. Mitchell was fun and exciting and his kisses were the stuff dreams were made of. He also understood my compulsion to solve crimes, even if I did it in a different way than he did. While he cared about my safety and asked me not to get involved in police matters, he also didn't use his position to try to force me to stay out of them. But Mitchell wasn't from Cherry Hill, and his job as a traveling detective meant he'd likely never be able to settle down here, if anywhere, for the long-term, even if he wanted to.

Marty was steady, stable, and kind. And as the manager of the hardware store two doors down from the diner, he wasn't going anywhere. He had lived in this small town his entire life and planned to do so until the day he died. Though he wasn't a fan of me getting involved in local police cases, he also understood why I did so and helped me deal with the emotional consequences those cases brought. Hopefully 1986 would be a crime-free year in Cherry Hill, so I wouldn't need him for that specific purpose any longer.

While I enjoyed fun and excitement, I was also starting to realize I wouldn't mind settling into a stable and steady life in my hometown. I dreamed of raising my family here, where my kids' grandparents would live a few streets away, and where I could spend time with Trixie and my aunt whenever I wanted. I was about to turn twenty-nine, and I would prefer to get married and start having kids sooner rather than later.

"What does Starla think about it?" Trixie asked, speaking about my aunt.

"She's been surprisingly quiet about it."

I lived with Aunt Star, and she often gave me advice, but I figured she might be afraid that if she gave too much advice about this, I'd choose the guy she thought I should instead of making my own decision.

"And she's out of town now, right?"

"Yeah, she and Darren left Tuesday afternoon. They'll be back next Tuesday night."

My aunt had been dating Cherry Hill's new Chief of Police Darren Turley for about a year. Both of them were workaholics and rarely took a vacation, but I'd finally convinced Aunt Star to take a break from her real estate agency and take her man out of town. They were off on a Caribbean cruise, which meant they couldn't even call home to check on anything unless it was an emergency. It was probably driving both of them crazy that they didn't know what was happening here at home, but they needed to spend an extended period of quality time together where they couldn't be distracted or pulled away by work.

"So she can't help you figure this out," Trixie stated.

"No. But I need to do it on my own. It needs to be fully my decision."

"And you're not leaning one way or the other?" She took a sip of her coffee as she waited for my response.

"I don't know!" I closed my eyes and shook my head.

"Okay, let's try this. Tell me how you feel when you think of Mitchell."

I pictured his handsome face in my mind, and I couldn't help but smile. "I feel excited and happy and tingly."

Trixie chuckled. "I remember that feeling."

"You don't still get tingly when you think of Scott?" I teased as I opened my eyes.

"Oh, I do sometimes." She grinned at me. "But I also often feel annoyed or mad or flat-out irritated with him. That's what almost ten years of marriage and two kids will do for you." Her grin turned into a soft smile that showed she didn't regret those ten years, though.

"Well," I said, my smile fading, "I also have those negative feelings about Mitchell."

"Because of Chris?"

I nodded. Chris was Mitchell's lifelong best friend. I'd known about their friendship from the beginning of my relationship with Mitchell, but what I didn't know for a long time was that Chris was a woman, and the two of them dated for nearly a year and broke up just weeks before Mitchell met me. I discovered the truth at Christmas when Chris was in a terrible accident and Mitchell was forced to tell me the entire truth. He tried to tell me he didn't love her, but I could tell that wasn't true, even though he was desperately trying to convince himself it was.

"I can understand that," my best friend said. "And how do you feel when you think about Marty?"

I smiled again. "Warm and safe and happy."

Trixie nodded. "And tingly?"

My neck and face heated. "Yeah. And tingly, even though I've never kissed him." I put my hands on my cheeks. "I shouldn't feel tingly about two different men."

"Girl, before Scott, I felt tingly about lots of guys. There's nothing wrong with that. It's healthy."

"Yeah, but I was dating one guy and then discovered I felt tingly about another. That's not great."

"It's not terrible, either. It's not like you were married or engaged to Mitchell. You hadn't even officially been dating all that long. You're not going to feel like this about both of them forever. Trust me on this. Once you truly fall in love with and commit to one of them, that'll be it. That's not to say you won't ever think another man is attractive or even get tiny tingles for someone else, because you probably will due to the fact that you're human. But don't ever doubt that you're ultimately a one-man woman."

I nodded. "Okay, thanks. That makes me feel better."

"Good. Back to the guys, it seems one makes you feel excited, while the other makes you feel secure. Which of those is more important to you?"

I pushed the remnants of my decimated pancakes around my plate with my fork. "I've never felt secure with a man before." I didn't need to add that I never even felt fully secure with my former fiancé, Walter, because Trixie was well aware.

"Is that an answer or an observation?"

I tilted my head to the side. "An observation. I want some excitement—I can't deny that. But that can't be all there is. I need security and stability, too."

"And Mitchell doesn't provide that?"

"Not really. I never know—*he* never knows—where he'll be or for how long. Even though he says he'd like a more stable job at some point, he doesn't know when that will be or where it'll be. But we talked about where he might end up, and there's not enough opportunity here in Cherry Hill for him career-wise."

"So do you have your answer, then?" Trixie asked.

"I don't know. In so many ways, Marty makes more sense, but life with him won't be exciting. I know exactly what I'd be getting with him both now and for the rest of my life. With Mitchell, there's an element of mystery—of 'anything can happen'—that I like. And I do like Mitchell an awful lot, even despite the Chris thing." I covered my eyes with my hands. "Why? Whyyyyy am I in this position where I have to choose?"

"Choose what?" Callie Collison asked as she topped off Trixie's coffee and slid another Diet Coke across the table to me.

"Between her men," Trixie said to my aunt's best friend, who had figured out my predicament with the two men even though I hadn't explicitly told her. She was a perceptive woman.

"Yeah," Callie propped her fist on her waist. "That's a tough one. Too bad you can't have them both."

"Ha." I snorted. "As if either of them would share me."

Callie quickly looked around the diner and then sat down next to me. I scooted over in the booth to give her more room.

"You haven't heard from Mitchell since Christmas?" Callie asked.

"No, but I asked him not to contact me."

"So you don't know how he's feeling about that Chris woman?"

I sighed. "I don't. But I'm assuming if he decided he wanted her instead of me, he would let me know."

"And he hasn't been in town at all?"

"Nope." Mitchell lived in nearby Jefferson City, but there was no reason for him to visit Cherry Hill unless it was to see me or help out the police. "The police department doesn't need him anymore. Thanks to all the crazy crimes we had here last year, he's trained Darren, Frank, and the others to handle anything that happens from here on out."

As if on cue, a siren sounded in the distance, growing louder by the second. The three of us looked at each other in silence for a few seconds, and then Callie stood, hurried to the door, and stepped outside. Everyone in the diner watched her, knowing she'd fill us all in when she returned inside. When she didn't come back after a few seconds but instead raised her hand to her mouth, I jumped to my feet and made my way to the door as quickly as I could with my bum leg, courtesy of a fall out of a tree when I was a child. Most everyone else decided to follow.

When I exited The Check, two police cruisers were screeching to a stop on Main Street a few dozen yards shy of the diner—right in front of the hardware store. My hand went to my heart when I spied Marty sitting on the sidewalk with his back leaning against the front of the store. Though the sun had yet to rise, the streetlights and red-and-blue lights from the police cars illuminated him enough to reveal an ashen face and what appeared to be blood on his hands, knees, and tan Carhartt jacket.

Chapter Two

My heart leapt into my throat as I raced toward Marty, but Officer Jake Park reached him first and held out a hand to stop me.

I tried to push past the young man, but Interim Deputy Chief of Police Frank Nichols lightly gripped my shoulders to hold me back and said quietly, "He's not hurt, Becky. I promise. You need to let us talk to him first."

I was briefly annoyed by Frank's use of my childhood nickname, but then Marty's eyes met mine from a few yards away, and the anguish in them sent a bolt of pain through my chest.

"He needs me," I pleaded to Frank as tears filled my eyes.

"Maybe so, but you can't touch him or talk to him yet."

Frank gently turned me away as Marty slowly got to his feet and Jake ushered him toward the store's door. Over my shoulder, I watched Jake slip a pair of rubber gloves on before touching the door handle.

"Go back to The Check," Frank said to me in a kind voice and then said more loudly to the crowd behind me, "All of you, please go back inside. It's cold out here, and there's nothing we can tell you yet about what's happened."

I asked Frank, "Will you come get me when it's okay for Marty to talk to anyone else? Please? Promise me."

Frank nodded, compassion written all over his lined face. "Somebody will let you know. I promise."

Callie slipped an arm around my shoulders and said, "Come on, honey. Let's go back inside and wait."

"Callie?" Frank said before we walked away.

"Yes?"

"We'll need to talk to everyone who was in the diner. You don't have to keep them there if they need to get to work, but can you write down everyone's name and phone number for us?"

"Can do."

The diner was abuzz when Callie and I stepped back inside. She guided me back to my table, and when I was seated, she held up my soda to my mouth. "Drink. The cold will help with the shock."

I took a big gulp as Callie said, "I need to get that list made for Frank, but I'm here if you need me, okay?"

I nodded, and she patted my shoulder before she walked away.

"Trix," I said in a pained voice, "he had blood all over him." I took another drink of soda.

She nodded. "I saw. Did Frank say anything to you about what happened?"

"All he said is Marty isn't hurt." I took a deep breath. "*Somebody's* hurt, though. That much is obvious."

"But it was the police that came, not the ambulance," Trixie said. "What does that mean?"

Dread filled me when I realized the implication. "I'd say that means the other person is dead."

Trixie's eyes went wide. "Oh goodness, you're probably right." She sucked in a breath. "Do you think it's Todd?"

Todd Jones was a recent graduate of Cherry Hill High and had worked at the store for the past five or six months.

"I sure hope not." I put my drink down and placed my hand on my stomach. "I think I might be sick. I don't want to think about who might be lying in a pool of blood two doors down. Haven't we had enough murders around here in the past year?" Cherry Hill had two murders last year, which was two more than we'd had in the previous three decades.

"First of all, we don't know for sure someone's dead," Trixie said. "And second, even if they are, we don't know it's a murder. Maybe it was an accident. It's a hardware store. There's lots of dangerous tools and equipment in there."

"Yeah," I said, "but how could an accident happen overnight? It's not like the store was open. Whoever's in there probably shouldn't have been there. It's not uncommon for Marty to stay late or go in early to get some work done in the office, but nobody else should be there this early."

"Maybe Marty walked in on someone robbing the store."

"Again?" The store was robbed a few days before Christmas, and Marty was attacked when he happened upon the thieves.

Trixie replied, "I know it doesn't seem probable, but it could happen."

"But then why isn't Marty the one who's hurt? Why does he have someone else's blood all over him?" I truly felt like I was going to throw up now.

"I don't know, Beck."

Trixie slid her hand across the table to me, and I took it, surprised my usually hands-off friend was offering me physical comfort, but I was grateful she knew I needed it.

The bell over the diner door jingled, and I looked up, expecting to see a police officer, but instead my friend and former classmate, Kyle Korte, entered. His eyes scanned the room and then landed on me. He made a beeline for our table, sat down next to me, and slid an arm around my shoulders.

"You okay?"

"I honestly don't know."

Kyle nodded. "What do you know about what happened?"

"Nothing, except Marty was covered in blood, but he's not

hurt." I raised an eyebrow at him. "How did you know to come down here?"

"Callie called me," he explained. "She thought I'd want to know, and she asked me to call Marty's parents."

Kyle had been Marty's roommate for more than a year, so it made sense Callie would call him.

"Where are his parents?" Trixie asked. "Did the police let them in the store?"

He shook his head. "They're in Kansas City taking care of Karla's kids while she's out of town." Karla was Marty's younger sister, was in my class in school, and was Kyle's high school sweetheart. "I called Karla's house, and Henry said he'd head home as soon as he could, but the drive will take several hours."

"I hope he's okay," I whispered.

Kyle pulled me up tightly against him. "He will be, no matter what happened. Marty's a strong man. You know that."

"Yeah." I laid my head on his shoulder.

"You need me to distract you from thinking about what's happening down the street?" he asked.

"Yes, please."

An hour later, Trixie and Kyle both reluctantly headed off to work, and Veronica Coker, my friend and pastor's wife, joined me at The Check.

"I can't keep sitting here," I said to her after we'd waited nearly another hour. "I have to know what's going on."

"They're not telling anyone what's going on yet," Veronica said. "But if Frank said he'd let you know the minute you can talk to Marty, he'll follow through on that. You don't need to go anywhere."

I shook my head. "I need to go to work. I'm already late."

"I told Harold he's staying in the church office all day so you can deal with whatever this is."

Of course she did. And no doubt Pastor Coker would do exactly as his wife said.

"Unless you *want* to go to work," Veronica said. "Do you need to get out of here and think about something else?"

"No," I said. "At least I can't see the store from here. From the church office, I'd be able to see right through the store's front windows."

"Do you want to go home, then?" she asked. "I can go with you."

"No, Frank knows this is where I am." I patted the table. "I'm staying until he comes to get me."

"You can ask Callie to tell him you're at home."

"I'm staying."

She nodded as the bell over the door jingled again. People had been in and out all morning, so I didn't bother looking up until I realized the entire room had quieted, leaving only the low sound of Keith Whitley singing "Miami, My Amy" through the diner's speakers.

When I saw the man standing in the doorway this time, I froze. Everyone's eyes were on Detective Mitchell Crowe as his gaze focused on me.

"What's he doing here?" Veronica asked in a low voice.

In an instant, I knew the answer to her question, but I couldn't tear my eyes away from Mitchell. "He's here because Darren's *not* here." And Darren was going to be upset when he learned he was out of the country for the first major crime since he was named Police Chief four weeks ago after the former chief's sudden but not altogether surprising retirement.

"Oh. Makes sense."

Mitchell stalked across the restaurant to our table, his gaze locked on mine the entire way.

"You okay?" he asked gruffly.

"Honestly, no."

He nodded. "Let's talk outside."

I grabbed my coat and followed him out. As the door closed behind us, chatter started back up inside the diner.

"Down here." He took my hand and led me a few doors down in the opposite direction from the hardware store and far enough so nobody in the diner could see us. Then he wrapped his arms around me, and I sank into him.

"He's all right," Mitchell said against my hair, without me asking. "Physically, at least."

"Okay. Can you tell me what happened?" I pulled back from him but stayed close.

"From what he says, he got to work early, and he discovered John Kemper lying on the floor in a pool of blood."

I sucked in a lungful of frigid air. "Oh, no."

"You know John?"

"Of course. He owns the store, and he ran it until about six or seven years ago when he and his wife Margie moved to Springfield to be near their children's families. His wife passed away a couple years ago." My heart pounded. "Is John dead?"

Mitchell nodded. "Yeah."

"How did he die?"

"I can't tell you that yet. But it wasn't a natural death or an accident."

"Which is why you're here?"

"Yes."

"Because Darren's on a ship in the middle of the Caribbean."

"Yes." He fingered the end of one of my auburn curls. "And you need to stay out of this investigation."

I took a step back. "What?"

"You can't try to solve this one."

I narrowed my eyes at him. "Why not?"

"Because it involves Marty."

"It *involves* Marty?" I crossed my arms over my chest. "What's that supposed to mean?"

"You'll get too emotionally invested."

"Because Marty's boss died? It's not like I wasn't emotionally invested in all the other craziness that's happened in this town in the past year. Last time, Marty was a *victim*. As was I, if you recall."

"Please do this for me."

I moved my hands to my hips and jutted my chin out. "No."

"No?"

"No."

He ran his fingers through his short, dark hair. "Baby—"

"Don't you 'baby' me, Mitchell Crowe. I'm not your baby. And you know as well as I do that if Marty is *involved* in this—and I'm still not sure what that means—I'm going to do everything in my power to figure out who did it." I jabbed my finger at him. "You know *he* didn't do this, right?"

"Beckett—"

"Right?"

"No, I don't know that."

I'd heard the phrase "saw red" before, but this was my first time experiencing it. "Are you kidding me?"

Mitchell grasped my shoulders and I tried to twist away from him, but he held me still.

"Listen to me," he said. "Do I *think* he did it? No. Do I know for absolute certain he didn't do it? Also no. I'm a detective. I can't let my personal opinion of people affect how I do my job. I can't rule people out as suspects simply because they don't seem like killers."

My hands balled into fists. "Well, I'm glad to know Marty doesn't seem like a killer to you," I said, my voice dripping with sarcasm.

"Is this how it's going to be, then?" he asked.

"Is this how what's going to be?" I retorted, finally jerking out of his grasp.

"You're just going to take his side?" He folded his arms over his chest.

"If by that you mean do I *know* he's not a murderer, then yes, I'm taking his side. If you mean am I choosing him over you, the jury is still out. The two months isn't up yet. But I'll tell you right now that if you send Marty James to prison for a murder he didn't commit, you and I are done. *Forever.*"

He briefly closed his eyes and took a deep breath in through his nose. "Beckett, I have to do my job."

"I didn't realize your job required you to suspect good, innocent men of violent crimes."

"That's not what I'm saying. Stop twisting my words. And please try to see this from my point of view," he pleaded. "I don't like this situation any more than you do, but I have to stay impartial. We'll hopefully be able to rule Marty out as a suspect very quickly, but we have to go through the proper steps to do that. I could compromise the entire case, let alone lose my job, if I don't. I know you're worried and upset about all this, and I understand that. But I can't be who you think you need me to be right now. I can't do things your way, and I can't assure you everything will be okay, because I don't know that yet."

He wasn't wrong. I knew all that, but I didn't have to like it. "Fine."

Mitchell raised an eyebrow at me. "Fine, we'll do it my way? Or fine, we're done?"

"Fine, do what you need to do to catch the real killer," I took a deep breath, "who is not Marty."

He shot me a wry smile. "My first priority will be to rule him out."

"Thank you."

"You're welcome." He searched my eyes. "Are we okay?"

I sighed. "Yeah. I'm sorry I got so worked up."

"I get why you did. Come here."

Mitchell pulled me into his arms again, and I didn't resist as I slipped my arms around him and rested my head against his shoulder. It felt natural to be in his arms again, even if I was irritated with him.

"Detective Crowe!" Frank's voice reached us from down the street.

We both turned our heads toward the voice, and my heart sank when I spied Marty walking to one of the police cars next to the two officers, his face turned our way. I didn't need to be close enough to see his eyes to know they'd be filled with hurt at the sight of me in Mitchell's arms.

"I need to talk to him," I said to Mitchell as I pulled away from him, while still watching Marty. He didn't look away from me as he got into the front passenger seat of a police car. I hoped the fact that he wasn't handcuffed or being put into the back seat was a good sign.

Mitchell's hand wrapped around my elbow to keep me from heading down the street. "Not yet."

I turned to him in a panic. "They didn't arrest him, did they?"

Mitchell shook his head. "No. They're just taking him to the station to answer more questions."

"Does he have to stay in those bloody clothes while he answers questions?"

"No, and we'll need his clothes and shoes as evidence."

"I'll go get him some clean ones." That would give me something productive to do. "I'll bring them to the station."

"That doesn't mean you can see him when you get there."

I gave him a wavering grin. "You think I can't talk Frank into it?"

He chuckled. "I wouldn't put it past you—or Frank."

Chapter Three

"Frank, all I want to do is make sure Marty's okay," I explained to him in the police station lobby.

"And I'm telling you he is," Frank replied.

"There's no way he can be. Maybe he's not physically hurt, but he discovered his boss's dead body. And you know that's not the first body he's run across in the past year."

Nearly a year ago, I found the body of our mutual friend Aidan Patrick, and Marty arrived mere seconds later.

I continued, "I know from experience, nobody is okay after something like that. John wasn't just Marty's boss, but also his friend and mentor. And earlier you *promised* you'd let me talk to him."

"Frank, you know you're going to give in to her, especially since Detective Crowe isn't here at the moment to stop you." This came from Barbara Young, the front desk receptionist at the station. She usually didn't do anything to help me out, but she knew Frank well. "Just get it over with already so I don't have to watch this little melodrama play out any longer." She flicked a finger back and forth between the two of us.

Frank sighed and held out his hand. "Give me the clothes, and I'll come get you when he's changed."

I gave him a sunny smile and handed over the duffel bag of clothes I'd grabbed from Marty's house. Kyle was at work, but few people in Cherry Hill locked their doors during the day, so I'd had no trouble walking right into their house and getting everything I thought Marty might need. I'll admit I blushed when I opened his underwear drawer, but it had to be done.

"Where's Mitchell?" I asked Barbara after Frank disappeared into "the pit," the main open room of the station filled with officers' desks.

"Oh, no. I'm not telling you anything," the woman replied. "Just have a seat and wait for Frank."

I sank onto one of the cold, metal folding chairs in the wood-paneled lobby and thumbed through a well-worn copy of *Good Housekeeping* while I waited.

"You can come on back, Becky," Frank said several minutes later.

I followed him through the pit and toward one of the two small interview rooms. Marty stood from one of the wooden chairs when I entered, and Frank closed the door behind me, leaving the two of us alone. I rushed around the table and flung my arms around him.

"How are you?" I asked.

Marty snaked one arm around me to pull me tightly against him, and he tucked my head under his chin with his other hand. "I don't know."

We stood there holding each other in silence for at least a minute. I could feel the tension slowly leave his body and his heart rate slow down from its earlier frantic pace.

"Are you and Mitchell …?" Marty finally asked.

I tilted my head back to look up at him. "No. The hug was … well, a hug. He knew I was upset." I didn't go into detail about my conversation with Mitchell.

Marty nodded, cupped my cheeks in his hands, pressed his lips to my forehead, and let go of me.

The kiss, innocent as it may have been, left me stunned for a few seconds before I could take the chair Marty pulled out for me.

"Thanks for coming and for the clean clothes," he said from across the table.

"You're welcome." I took a deep breath, trying to ignore the lingering feeling of Marty's warm mouth on my skin. "Do you feel like telling me what happened?"

He took a deep breath and began, "I got to work early to get caught up on some bookwork. The back door was unlocked, which was strange. I always lock up, and since the robbery, I make sure to double check. But the lock didn't look tampered with, and Madge Conley comes in to clean on Wednesday nights, so I assumed she accidentally left it unlocked. When I went inside, I had my guard up a little. Everything looked fine as I walked down the main aisle, but then when I headed up the stairs to go to the office, I glanced down through the other aisles, and ..." He choked up.

I slid a hand across the table, and he took it in his larger, callused hand.

"And what?" I asked gently.

"And I saw him ... John." His hand squeezed mine. "He was lying in a pool of blood." He took a gulp of air. "I didn't know it was him at first. Only a few lights were on, he was facedown, and I couldn't see much of him from my vantage point. I ran back down the stairs and to ... his body." He looked down at the table, but his face radiated pain. "I know I shouldn't have touched him, but I wasn't thinking about it being a crime scene at the time. I thought ... I guess I thought he'd fallen or something. I knelt down and checked for a pulse, but there was no doubt he was dead."

I squeezed his hand and waited for him to compose himself.

"I don't know why he was there," he said. "He shouldn't have been there. Yesterday afternoon he called and told me he was coming to town for a few days, but there was no reason for him to come to the store that early, especially since he couldn't have known I'd be there early today."

"Can you tell me how he died? Could you tell?"

Marty visibly swallowed and said, "The back of his head was bashed in. And there was a bloody axe on the floor near him."

I suppressed a shudder and tried not to visualize the scene.

"Did you touch the axe?" I asked.

"No."

"Good."

"Once I was able to think clearly enough, I went to the phone at the checkout counter and called the police station. And then I went outside, because I just couldn't be in there alone with him." He swallowed again and looked directly into my eyes. "Beckett, do they think I did this? Is that why I'm still here ... why they haven't told me I can go home?"

I shook my head. "I don't think anyone in this town will ever think you did it. But you found the body, so they have to consider you a suspect. If they didn't, when they go to trial with the real murderer, the defense attorney could make a big stink about it and possibly call for a mistrial. So they have to do this the right way. But you didn't do it, so the evidence will prove it wasn't you."

"But what if it doesn't?" A hint of fear appeared in his eyes. "Nobody broke in. Nothing seemed to be missing from the store, so it's not a suspected robbery. I found the body. His blood was all over me. And even though I didn't touch the axe today, I almost certainly unpacked it or hung it on the rack, so my finger-prints will be on it. That all points to me doing it."

"But why would you do it?" I spread my hands wide. "You have no motive. You loved him like a son would. And you don't gain anything from his death." I paused. "Do you?"

"No. In fact, if his kids decide to sell the store and the new owners want to run it themselves, I might be out of a job." The fear in his eyes intensified. "I've never worked anywhere else. I started working there part-time when I was fourteen. What am I going to do?"

"That's the worst case scenario. Try not to focus on that, since we don't know what'll happen."

Marty tapped his fingernails on the table. "They've gone out to search my house. They don't have a warrant, but I said they could do it. I don't know what they're looking for, but they're not going to find anything tying me to the murder, because I didn't do it." He shook his head. "Do you think I need a lawyer? Frank told me I could have one before they started asking me questions, but I didn't see the need, since I'm innocent. But now I'm not sure what to do."

"I think that might be good. Do you have a lawyer?"

"No, I've never needed one."

"Okay, which of the three lawyers in town do you want me to call for you?" I asked.

"You'd do that?"

"Of course. Do you want Hank, Nancy, or Donnie?"

"Donnie. I've been to his office a few times to deal with things for John. He also plays poker with my dad."

"Done. I'll call him as soon as I leave here. And don't answer any more questions or even chit-chat with any of the officers unless Donnie is with you." I tapped my lips with my pointer finger. "In fact, if you haven't been arrested or charged with anything, I don't think they can make you stay here, so I'm taking you with me when I go."

Marty's eyebrows raised. "Really?"

"Really." I stood. "Let's go."

He followed me out the door, and when I got to the middle of the pit, I stopped and said loudly to the room, "Since Marty hasn't been arrested or charged with any crime, and since you don't seem to have any more questions for him at the moment, he's leaving. If there's a legal reason he can't go, you have until we walk out the door to stop him."

Nobody said a word as we walked out of the pit, through the

lobby, and out into the cold sunshiny day. We both got into my yellow Ford Pinto, and as I cranked the engine I asked, "Do you want me to take you to your truck or to Donnie's office?"

"Might as well start with Donnie's office. That is, if you're willing to go with me."

"I'm sorry, Marty, but I can't represent you," Donnie Masters said from behind his massive mahogany office desk.

"Why?" I questioned.

"Because I'm the executor of John's estate." Donnie folded his hands over his ample belly. "It would be a conflict of interest."

"But I'm not in his family," Marty said. "The estate doesn't matter to me."

Donnie leaned forward and steepled his fingers. "I'm not at liberty to divulge details to you at this point," he said, "but considering the contents of the will, the estate *does* matter to you."

My eyes widened, and when I glanced over at Marty, his facial expression reflected my own.

"John left something to me?" Marty asked.

"As I said, I'm not at liberty to say."

"But if Marty wasn't left anything, the estate wouldn't matter to him, right?" I prompted.

"I can't say." Donnie obviously wasn't going to offer any precise information.

"Have the police seen the will?" I asked.

"They'll need a warrant first." The man shrugged. "But they'll get one soon enough."

I bit the inside of my lip. "And the contents of the will are going to give Marty a possible motive for killing John?"

"I can't answer that specifically," Donnie said. "But anyone named in the will would potentially have a motive for killing John."

"Okay," Marty said. "Sounds like I'm going to need a good lawyer."

"Maybe so," Donnie said. "I'll call Nancy and tell her you're on your way over."

"We'll do everything we can to get you cleared as soon as possible," Nancy Milligan said to Marty from across her office desk. "Nobody is really going to believe you did this, but you'll be the prime suspect until concrete evidence is found against someone else."

"Is it going to be a problem if I try to solve this case?" I asked Nancy.

Marty replied before she could. "It's a problem with me. I don't want you getting hurt because of me."

I shook my head. "First of all, you didn't do anything. Second of all, I'm not letting you go to jail for something you didn't do." I pursed my lips. "And I don't think you want to know what'll happen if you try to stop me."

The corners of Marty's mouth tilted down as Nancy chuckled.

She said, "I can't exactly endorse your plan, Beckett, but if you're going to investigate, make sure you don't compromise any evidence in the process. And this should go without saying, but I'm going to say it anyway. Don't do anything dumb and get yourself hurt or killed." Nancy looked at Marty. "And don't you say anything to anybody about this, other than your closest friends and family. Don't meet with or talk to the police again without me. Got it?"

Marty nodded. "Yes, ma'am."

"Good. I have everything I need from you for now. Call me if you think of anything else that might be relevant, and I'll keep you apprised of anything I find out."

Marty and I stood, and he reached out to shake Nancy's hand.

"Thanks, Nancy."

"Of course. We'll get you exonerated in no time."

"You want me to come to your house with you?" I asked Marty when I pulled my car up next to his pickup in the parking lot behind the hardware store after meeting with Nancy.

"I do, but ..." He looked away from me.

"But what?"

"But we're not dating. I'm thankful for all you've done for me today, but you need to step away. This mess has put you in the middle between me and Mitchell once again, and it's going to skew your view of both of us. I don't want you to choose me because you feel sorry for me or because he's simply doing his job and is forced to arrest me. Plus, you don't want to choose me anyway. I might go to prison." He drew in a shaky breath. *"Prison. For murder."*

As he spoke, my heart began to pound, and my breathing grew shallow. "You're not going to prison!"

"If there's anything I've learned from you in the past year, it's that a criminal needs means, motive, and opportunity. And it seems I have all three, even though I still don't know what my motive is. I didn't do this, but it sure looks like I did."

"I'm going to find the real killer, Marty."

"No. You can't. This person killed once, and they may well kill again. You can't put yourself in danger for me."

I narrowed my eyes at him. "I can put myself in danger for anybody I want, thank you very much. And I choose to put myself in danger for you." I poked him in the shoulder to emphasize my point.

"Don't."

"You can't stop me."

"Beckett," he pleaded.

I folded my arms across my chest. "I'm not letting you go to prison, Marty James, and that's that."

Chapter Four

"Can you take a break?" I asked my mom at her teller window at Cherry County Bank.

She glanced over at Aggie at the next window, who nodded at Mom and then smiled at me.

"You okay, Beckett?" Aggie asked.

"It's been a crazy day," I replied instead of giving her a direct answer.

"That's what I've heard."

Mom locked her cash drawer and then led me across the lobby toward the hall where the break room was located. When we were almost to the hallway, a male voice called out my name. I stopped and turned toward Jeff Jenkins, the bank's vice-president and my high school boyfriend, who was standing in his office doorway with his hands in his suit pockets.

"Have you talked to Marty?" he asked.

"Yeah."

"He all right?"

"As well as can be expected, I guess."

"Anything I can do to help?" he asked.

I shook my head. "No ... well, maybe." I remembered Jeff's

older brother dated John's daughter Kathleen in high school. He might have some insight into the family. I wished I'd asked Marty about John's kids, but I doubted he'd tell me anything negative about either of them.

"You two want to come in here and talk?" He jerked his head toward his office.

"Sure."

Mom followed me in and Jeff closed the door behind us before settling into his chair.

"Tell us everything you know," Mom demanded of me.

I told them everything related to the case and nothing related to my potential relationships.

"Is Marty home alone?" Jeff asked me.

I checked my watch. "His dad should be here by now. He was coming from Kansas City."

"Okay, I'll call his house here in a little bit to see how he's doing."

"You're good enough friends with him to do that?" I asked.

"I am." He smirked at me. "I seem to recall a little birdie telling me I should get to know him several months back."

"Oh." I nodded and shot him a soft smile. "Yeah. I did. I'm glad you're friends. Anyway, tell me what you know about John's kids." I looked from Jeff to Mom. "Both of you."

"You think one of them did it?" Mom asked.

"Well, it wasn't Marty. We've got to find other people who had a motive."

Jeff said, "I'm guessing I'd be wasting my breath if I suggested you stay out of this investigation for the sake of your safety?"

"You would."

"Okay, I won't say it, then."

"I would say it, but I also know it wouldn't do any good," Mom said.

"Back to the topic at hand," I said. "Tell me about Kathleen."

"You might remember my brother dated her back in the day,"

Jeff began. "What you might not know is that right after they graduated high school, he proposed, and she said no. Within six months she was married to someone else and living in Springfield. They divorced the following year, and then she married again a few years later. Jamie was gutted."

"Why did Kathleen say no when Jamie proposed?" Mom asked.

"Said she wanted bigger things than what Jamie and a small town could give her."

"Wow," I said. What I didn't say was that's exactly why Marty's wife divorced him several years back, and it was a potential reason why I might decide to not date him.

"I guess it's good she decided that before they got married," he said. "I'm not sure Jamie ever really got over her, though. I think that might be why his marriage didn't work out."

"Does Kathleen work? And what does her husband do?" I asked. "Do either of you know?"

"I don't think she works," Jeff said. "Her husband is in advertising, I believe. Or at least he was back then. He's quite a bit older than her. Eight or ten years, maybe."

I nod. "And what do either of you know about John's son Paul?"

"He also lives in Springfield," Mom said. "Married, has a couple teenage kids. Last I knew, he was working at a sporting goods store. If he was going to work in a store, I'm not sure why he didn't want to stay here and run the hardware store."

"I know why," Jeff said, "but you can't tell anyone this. Well, maybe other than the police. Marty told me in confidence, but I feel comfortable telling you two under the circumstances. I have a feeling this information might help out his case now, but I doubt Marty will say anything about it."

Mom and I both assured him we wouldn't spread the news to anyone who didn't need to know.

Jeff said, "Paul stole from the store."

My eyes widened. "What?"

He nodded. "John caught him taking cash out of the register a couple times when he was a teenager. Then after he moved away, things would disappear from the store when Paul was in town for visits. John finally banned his son from the store and changed the locks."

"I have to tell Mitchell about this," I said.

"I figured you would," Jeff said. "I was going to call you about it tonight if I didn't see you today."

"Do either of you know anyone else who might have a reason to kill John and frame Marty for it?" I asked. "Because it seems like a set-up to me."

"Everybody loves Marty," Jeff stated. "Well, except maybe Mitchell." He shot me a wry grin. "And there was that one time *you* suspected him of murder."

I groaned and hid my face in my hands. "Am I ever going to live that down?" I look back at Jeff. "How did you know about that, anyway?"

"Marty told me."

"Of course he did. Tell me again why I said you two should be friends?"

Jeff chuckled. "Speaking of Mitchell, I haven't seen him around since Christmas. You two still together?"

My eyes darted to my mother before focusing back on Jeff. "Marty didn't tell you?"

Jeff twisted his lips. "He told me. I just wanted to see how you'd answer that question."

"Ah. No, we're not together right now."

Jeff nodded. "He's a good guy. And so is Marty."

"I know," I said with a sigh.

"I need to talk to Mitchell," I said to Barbara Young in the police station lobby.

"No can do, Becky." Barbara didn't give me an explanation.

"Why not? It's about the case."

"You can't talk to him because he's not here."

"Oh?"

Barbara folded her arms over her chest. "And I'm not telling you where he is, either."

"Can you give him a message to call me?"

"I'm not your dating service," she replied.

I kept myself from sighing. "This has nothing to do with our relationship and everything to do with the murder. Do you want Marty to rot in jail forever for a crime he didn't commit?"

She pursed her lips, and I could tell my words had gotten to her. "Fine," she said. "I'll tell Detective Crowe to call you. Now head on out so I can get some work done."

"Can I talk to Frank?" I asked. "Or Jake?"

"Nope. They're busy. If you want them to prove Marty didn't do this, you'll leave them alone and give them time to do so. Now scoot. I said I'd tell Detective Crowe to call you, and I'm a woman of my word."

As I drove away from the station, I realized I'd left myself no option but to go home, since that's where Mitchell would be calling me. When I got there, I made a quick call to Veronica, who said she'd come over to keep me company.

When she arrived, we sat on the couch and she helped me fold laundry while I told her everything I'd learned from Marty and Jeff.

"I've discovered something, too," she said as she placed a folded washcloth on the stack teetering precariously on the coffee table.

"Oh, yeah?"

"Of course. I'm not letting you solve this crime alone. We're a package deal, remember?" She waved a hand towel at me and gave me a big smile.

"I remember." I mirrored her grin. "Lay it on me. What did you find out?"

"After you left for the police station, I went home and called Minnie Jensen."

"You what?!" I dropped the T-shirt I was in the process of folding.

Minnie was one of the town's biggest busybodies. She was also an atheist, so Veronica viewed her with a large dose of skepticism.

"I don't especially like the woman, but she always knows what's happening in this town, and she's lived here her entire life," Veronica explained.

"Why didn't you call Suzanne instead?" Suzanne LaHaye was the church's choir director and one of Veronica's closest friends. She was framed for one of the crimes last year, and she was a victim in the spate of burglaries at Christmas.

Veronica shrugged. "I tried calling her, but she didn't answer, so then I tried Minnie. She always gives us good tips, and I figured why not pump her for information?"

"And ...?" I prompted, momentarily forgetting about the laundry.

"She was all in a tizzy about John. Seems they grew up together. Anyway, once she calmed down a bit, I asked her to think about anyone who might want to hurt him. She said Kathleen's husband was fired from his job about six months ago."

"Did she know why?"

"No, John never heard a good explanation."

"How did Minnie find out about it?" I asked.

"She keeps in touch with John. She and Margie were friends."

"Okay," I pursed my lips as I thought, "so Kathleen and her husband are probably having money issues."

"I would assume so." Veronica added another washcloth to the stack.

"And an inheritance could come in handy for them."

"Yep. Minnie also said John was sued about fifteen years ago."

"Sued? I don't remember that."

"Well, you would've been a teenager, so I doubt you'd have known about it. I didn't know, either, but that was before our time here. Anyway, a man named Hugh Canby from Taylorville tripped over a ladder in the store, and he broke his arm. It didn't heal right, and he couldn't do his job at the factory anymore. He sued John, and he lost."

"So this guy might still have it out for John after fifteen years?"

Veronica pursed her lips. "I know it seems unlikely, but it's something to look into. The more possible suspects we can come up with, the better for Marty."

Brrrring!

I jumped up and rushed into the kitchen to answer the phone. "Hello?"

"Hi."

My heart beat a little faster at the sound of Mitchell's voice. "Hi."

"Barbara said you needed to talk to me about the case?"

"Yeah. I don't know if Marty told you this, but John's son Paul used to steal from the store, and John banned him and changed the locks."

Mitchell was silent for a few seconds. "How do you know this?"

"I got it from a source."

"A source, huh?"

"Yep. Did Marty tell you about that?"

Mitchell sighed. "No."

"I didn't figure. He doesn't like to talk badly about people."

"He needs to in this situation. He needs all the help he can get."

"I know. Also, John's son-in-law got fired from his job six months ago and is still unemployed. And about fifteen years ago, John was sued by Hugh Canby from Taylorville. Hugh lost. You might want to look into that, as well."

"You got all that from one source?"

"Two, actually."

"Is one of them named Suzanne?"

I chuckled. "Great guess, but no. Anyway, did you know any of that?"

"Frank told me about the lawsuit, but the other stuff is new info."

"Good." I considered asking him about the will, but I didn't want to put any focus on it since it seemed Marty had inherited something. I didn't want to provide any potential motive for him.

Mitchell said, "I'll ask Marty about the stuff you mentioned and see if there's anything he can add."

"He should be at his house right now, if you want to call there. No, wait. You need to call Nancy Milligan. She's his lawyer."

"I know, and I don't need to call him. He's here."

My hand flew to my chest. *"What?* Did you arrest him?"

"No, we asked him to come back to the station to talk about the will. He and Nancy are in the interview room while we decide what we need to do."

"Decide what you need to do about what?" I demanded. "Arresting an innocent man for murder?"

"Beckett—"

"Whether or not Marty was named in that will, he did *not* do this." I jabbed the air with my pointer finger, as if Mitchell could see me.

"I can't comment."

Veronica appeared in the kitchen doorway and raised her eyebrows at me before taking a seat at the kitchen table.

"Mitchell Eugene Crowe, you will tell me this instant what that will said, or I'll make sure you regret it until the day you die."

He snorted. "Are you threatening a police officer?"

"Indeed I am. Are you going to arrest me for it?"

"You know I'm not."

"Then tell me if Marty inherited something." I wrapped the phone cord so tightly around my finger it hurt.

Mitchell sighed. "Fine. You'll find out soon enough anyway. He got the store."

I let go of the phone cord, and it unraveled from my finger. "The store? The *hardware* store?"

Veronica's mouth gaped open.

"What other store would it be?" Mitchell replied.

My eyes narrowed. "Don't be a smart aleck. But why didn't John leave it to his kids?"

"You just gave me a very good reason why he didn't leave it to his son."

"Marty had no idea John left the store to him." I jabbed the air again. "I hope you realize that."

"I'll admit he seemed legitimately shocked when we told him."

"Well, then?" I propped my free hand on my hip.

"It's motive, Beckett. And we can't prove he didn't know."

"Maybe not, but if *he* didn't know, then John's kids probably didn't know, either, which gives them motive. Actually, they have motive whether they knew or not. One of them might've killed their dad because they needed money and thought they'd inherit the store and whatever else he owned. Or, on the other hand, they killed him because they found out he didn't leave the store to them and were angry about it."

"Or maybe neither of John's kids killed him," Mitchell stated.

"But why would Marty kill him, even if he did know—*which he didn't?*"

"Maybe he's having money trouble."

I let out a low scream. "He is not."

"You don't know that. And I need to go before you get any more irritated with me. Thanks for the info. We'll look into it."

The dial tone startled me, and I moved the phone in front of my face and stared at it for a few seconds. Then I hung it back up on the wall harder than I ever had and turned to Veronica, who had a grim look on her face.

"He didn't even say goodbye, the—"

Veronica held a hand up to stop me. "Don't say it. You'll regret it."

"I won't regret it." I sighed. "But I won't say it, either. That's not me. I won't let this mess change who I am."

Chapter Five

Within seconds, the phone rang again. I plucked it back off the wall, hoping Mitchell was calling to apologize for hanging up on me.

"Hello?" I said in a terse tone.

"Uh, Beckett? Are you all right?" Kyle's voice said down the line.

I sighed. "Yeah. Well, not really, but you know what I'm saying."

"Sure. Hey, I just got home from work, and Marty's dad is here. He's pretty upset, as you can imagine. He said they called Marty back to the station an hour or so ago to ask him more questions, and Marty wouldn't let him go along. Henry doesn't really know what's going on, and I don't either. Do you have an update? Have you talked to Mitchell?"

"I just talked to him, and I probably know more than anyone else does. I don't want to tie up the phone, though, in case Mitchell tries to call again or somebody else calls me with information. Can Henry come over here? You're welcome, too."

"Hang on a sec." He came back on a few seconds later. "Yeah, Henry's coming. What are you doing for dinner? You want me to pick you something up from The Blue Barn on my way?"

I looked at the clock. "Oh, I didn't realize what time it was, and I never stopped to eat lunch today. Food would be great. Mrs. Coker's here, so she might want something, too."

Veronica shook her head and stood from the table. "Tell him not to get anything for me. I need to be getting home to Harold."

"Never mind," I said to Kyle, "she's leaving. But grab me a burger and fries, please."

I said goodbye and hung up the phone with a sigh. "This is all such a mess."

"It is," Veronica agreed, "but we'll figure it out. We always do." She put her coat on. "Now, make sure you call me if you hear anything else, and I'll do the same. You'll be okay on your own until Henry and Kyle get here?"

"I will," I assured my friend. "Thanks for spending so much time with me today."

She had barely stepped out the door when the phone rang yet again. This time it was Edna Thorn, editor of *The Cherry Hill Standard*, our local weekly newspaper.

"Beckett, tell me what you know about this murder."

"You won't print any of what I tell you unless I approve it first, right?" I asked.

"Of course. And since we don't send next week's paper off to the printer until Monday, hopefully the killer will be caught by then."

"True. And if I tell you what I know, you'll also tell me what you know?" I countered.

"I will. If anybody's gonna solve a murder in this town, it's you."

My cheeks heated at the praise. "Well, I hope I'm able to. Here's what I know …" I then told her everything I thought was pertinent.

Then I asked, "What can you tell me that I don't already know?"

"Well, I'm not sure you'll believe me, but I don't know anything you didn't just tell me."

I sighed. "I believe you, but I wish it weren't true. We need some concrete evidence against someone other than Marty."

"I'll keep digging," Edna said. "Don't you worry."

"I stopped by the police station to see if they'd tell me anything, and of course they didn't," Henry James said as he stepped across the threshold into the house. "And I told them to let Marty know that if he can't find me when he leaves the station, to try here."

I took Mr. James' coat and hung it in the coat closet. "Can I hug you, Mr. James?" I asked.

He opened his arms wide, and I stepped into them. He held me tightly and I squeezed him back.

"Thanks for caring about my boy," he said. "And please, call me Henry."

When we finally let go of each other, I led him into the kitchen.

"What would you like to drink?" I asked. "We've got Coke and Diet Coke and water. Or I can make some coffee or tea."

"Coke is good," he said. "I have a feeling I'm going to need the caffeine."

I poured some Coke from the two-liter bottle into an ice-filled cup and placed it in front of him. Then I poured myself some Diet Coke and sat across from him at the glass-topped kitchen table.

"I'm so sorry about what's happening with Marty," I said. "And I'm sorry about John. You two were friends, right?"

Henry nodded. "We've known each other since we were little tykes. We haven't talked much since he moved away, but Marty keeps me updated." His face fell. "Kept me updated, I guess."

"Yeah. Are you okay with waiting until Kyle gets here for me to tell you what I know? Or do you want me to go ahead and tell you?"

His hands closed around his cup as he thought about his

answer. "Why don't you tell me anything Kyle might already know?"

I was only partway through my story when the doorbell rang. The door opened before I could stand, and Kyle's voice called out, "It's just me. And I'm locking the door behind me. Can't be too careful right now."

He appeared in the doorway holding a greasy paper bag. He plopped it on the table, and I stood to get him a drink along with silverware, condiments, and paper plates. I didn't figure I'd feel like doing dishes tonight.

"Did you hear anything interesting while you were at The Blue Barn?" I asked Kyle after we settled in with our meals.

"I did," he said around a bite of his burger. "Minnie Jensen was there, and she said she saw Kathleen pull into the police station parking lot an hour or so ago."

"That's not all that surprising." I popped a fry into my mouth and chewed as I thought. "I wonder about Paul. I guess he wasn't with her, or Minnie would've said."

"The rumor is he was in town earlier this afternoon," Kyle said. "That came from Carl Higgins, who heard it from Wayne Cooper."

Wayne Cooper owned and directed Cooper's Funeral Home, the only mortuary in town.

"I guess Wayne would know," Henry said. "Speaking of things people should know, where's Darren? Marty only mentioned Frank and Detective Crowe when he told me what they asked him at the station earlier."

"He and my aunt are on a Caribbean cruise," I replied. "I was hoping the police wouldn't try to track him down and bring him home for this, since Mitchell was available to be here. The two of them really need this time away together. But now I wish Darren was here to get Marty out of this mess."

Henry's eyebrows raised. "You don't trust your boyfriend to figure out who really did it, so they'll leave my son alone?"

I looked down at my plate. Did I trust Mitchell? I knew he was a good detective, but he also wasn't Marty's biggest fan. I was a little afraid his personal feelings might get in the way of doing everything he could to prove Marty's innocence, but I couldn't tell Henry that.

"He's not my boyfriend," I said as I looked Henry in the eye. "Not anymore. He's a good detective, but he doesn't know Marty. I'm pretty sure he doesn't think Marty killed John, but since he doesn't know what kind of man Marty is firsthand, he might not fully believe it. Darren would know without a doubt that Marty isn't capable of hurting anyone, much less murdering them."

"When will Darren and Starla be home?" Kyle asked.

"Next Tuesday."

"Five days is a long time in a situation like this," Henry said. "Marty could be in jail by then, if they don't find the real killer."

I groaned and dropped my head into my hands. "I know. I don't know what to do. I doubt the police will try to contact Darren, but I don't know if *I* should or not. Aunt Star was afraid something like this would happen to ruin their first big trip together. I don't want to do that to them, but I also don't want Marty to be thrown into prison."

"Well," Kyle said, "he wouldn't be in an actual prison by that point—just the county jail. Not that jail is great, but it's not as grim as you might be thinking." He pointed a fry at me. "And yes, I know you know that, but I wanted to point it out. Anyway, even if we contacted Darren, it would be days before he could get back. We might be able to solve this murder ourselves before then. Let's focus on that."

I took a deep breath and nodded. "Okay, here's what I know."

Ding-dong!

The ringing doorbell cut into the end of our discussion of the day's events. I stood, and so did Kyle.

He waved me back to my seat. "Let me get it. It's dark out,

and there's a killer on the loose. I doubt he or she would ring the doorbell, but I'd better answer just in case."

I nodded and sat back down, sending up a silent prayer of thanks for having so many people who had my back.

Seconds later, the door opened, and Marty's voice filtered in. I let out a long, relieved breath and looked at Henry, who was doing the same. We hadn't said it, but I knew we were both worried Marty wouldn't be allowed to leave the police station tonight.

We both stood as the men entered the room, and when Marty's eyes immediately sought me out, I smiled and headed toward him. Then I thought better of hugging him, considering our audience, and said, "I'm so glad you're here."

Henry reached his hand out to his son, and Marty took it but then hauled his dad toward him and pulled him into a hug. The surprise on Henry's face revealed the two didn't typically embrace, but he held his son even more tightly than he'd held me earlier.

The two men finally stepped apart, and Kyle plucked up his keys from where he'd dropped them on the counter earlier. He said to Marty, "I'll go get you some dinner. What do you want?"

"DQ is fine," Marty said as he dropped down into a chair. "A footlong chili dog and fries." He sighed. "And a chocolate shake. Thanks, man."

"Can you bring me a Dilly Bar?" I asked Kyle as Henry and I retook our seats.

"Will do. Henry? You need any ice cream?"

"Get me a banana split." Henry patted his belly. "What the missus doesn't know won't hurt her."

Marty laughed at that, which made me smile.

"Don't wait for me to get back to start talking about what happened at the police station," Kyle said as he headed for the front door. "I can catch up later. And I'm locking the door behind me."

"You ready to talk," I asked Marty, "or do you need a break?"

He sighed again. "I need a break." The dark circles under his eyes revealed the toll this day had taken on him. "In more ways than one," he added in a weary tone.

"You really do." I stood. "What do you want to drink? Something to keep you awake or help you sleep?"

Marty's fingers tapped on the tabletop. "I don't think sleep will be on the agenda for tonight, but I won't know if I don't try, so no caffeine."

"Sleepytime tea it is, then," I said as I pulled the teakettle out of the cabinet. I filled it with water and set it on the stove to heat.

To give Marty the break he asked for, I regaled him and his dad with a story about a three-year-old who interrupted the sermon on Sunday with a well-timed question that made Pastor Coker laugh and deeply embarrassed the child's parents.

Then, as I fixed the tea, Henry told us all the activities he and his wife did with the grandkids in Kansas City.

Finally, Marty's dad asked, "You hanging in there, son?"

"I guess. I didn't do it, and I'm pretty sure everyone at the station knows I didn't do it, but there's not much they can do about the evidence and my potential motive."

"You ready to talk about it now?" I asked.

"Might as well wait 'til Kyle gets back," Marty said.

Ding-dong.

"Speak of the devil," Henry said with a grin as he pushed out of his chair. "I'll get it."

As soon as he was out of the room, I reached my hand across the table to Marty. He took it in his own and squeezed.

"Thanks for everything you're doing," he said.

Before I could answer, we heard Henry's voice asking, "And who might you be, young lady?"

I let go of Marty's hand and took off to the front door, wondering if one of the girls from the church youth group had stopped by. Henry stepped to the side as I approached, revealing a

41

pretty blonde teenager with tear-stained cheeks on my front porch.

"Cynthia!" I exclaimed. "What are you doing here?"

Chapter Six

I reached out and pulled my cousin into the house before peeking outside. "Where are your parents?" I asked her.

"They're in Peoria visiting Leslie." Cynthia's older sister was a newspaper reporter in Peoria, Illinois.

I closed the door before hugging her. Out of the corner of my eye, I watched Henry sneak back to the kitchen.

"Is Aunt Star here?" Cynthia asked in a teary voice as she lay her head on my shoulder.

"No, honey, she and Darren are on a cruise." I stroked her hair. "She's gone 'til Tuesday. What's going on? Why are you here?"

"Thomas broke up with me," she said with a sniffle. "During seventh hour. Can you believe it? I was staying with Karen while my parents are out of town, but Karen never liked Thomas ... well, I think she actually *really* liked Thomas and was jealous. She just didn't like that he was dating me instead of her. She's always going on and on about how much he looks like Corey Haim. But anyway, I couldn't stay there with her and I didn't want to be at home alone. So I went home and packed a bag and drove up here." She finally pulled out of my arms and looked at me with sad eyes.

"You drove up here by yourself from Arkansas?" I asked. "In the dark?"

"It wasn't dark when I started," she said.

"No, I guess not. Anyway, now you're here." And what was I going to do with her? We were trying to solve a murder! The framed suspect was in the next room, and as much as I hated to admit it, I was maybe in danger, too, since I was trying to solve the crime, and everybody in town would know it based on my history.

"Hey, who was that man who opened the door?" Cynthia asked as she shrugged out of her Oakville High School letterman jacket, revealing a baggy Esprit sweatshirt over her acid-washed jeans. Then her eyes opened wide and she whispered, "Are you dating a much older man? Is he your sugar daddy?"

I couldn't help but laugh at the combination of fascination and horror in her tone. "No, he's my friend Marty's dad. Marty's in the kitchen too. Here, have a seat on the couch for a minute while I tell you what's going on, and then we'll call your parents to let them know you're here."

As I gave her the *Reader's Digest* condensed version of the day's events, the doorbell rang again. Then the door opened and Kyle stepped inside with some Dairy Queen bags.

"Why wasn't the door locked?" he demanded before spotting us on the couch. "Oh. Hi." He then turned on his trademark charm, placed the bags on the coffee table, held out his hand to Cynthia, and said, "I'm Kyle. Nice to meet you. I haven't seen you around here before."

I smacked his hand away. "This is my cousin Cynthia, and she's seventeen, so she's off limits. Put the flirting on the back burner and take Marty's food to him. But first, give me my Dilly Bar, and give Cynthia whatever ice cream you got for yourself."

"I would be honored to give Miss Cynthia my hot fudge sundae," he said with a small bow.

"Stop it," I ordered. "It's gross that you're flirting with a high schooler. I don't care if you're kidding or not—just don't."

"Yes, ma'am," Kyle said, finally dropping the grin and handing over our ice cream.

"I'll be in the kitchen in a few minutes," I told him. "Thank the guys for waiting, will you?"

"Aye, aye, captain." Kyle saluted me before snatching up the bags and heading into the kitchen.

Twenty minutes later, my living room was packed to the gills. After calling my cousin Leslie to let her and her parents know Cynthia was in Cherry Hill, I rang my parents to tell them their niece was in town and to ask if she could spend the next couple of nights with them, since I didn't feel it was safe for her to stay with me. Of course Mom and Dad agreed, and when Dad arrived to pick Cynthia up, Mom was with him. Unsurprisingly, she wanted an update on the murder.

I felt bad for Marty, as he hated being the center of attention, but it couldn't be helped. And I figured the more people who knew what was happening, the better. I was a little wary of having my teenage cousin in the room and getting her involved, but again, there wasn't much I could do about it. If I sent her upstairs, she'd probably listen in anyway. She was intrigued by the little I told her earlier.

"Marty," I said from my spot next to him in the middle of the couch, "why don't you tell us what happened at the station tonight, and we'll go from there?"

"Okay." Marty leaned forward and put his elbows on his knees. "First, they told me about the will. Apparently, John changed it just a few weeks ago and left the store to me." He dropped his head into his hands for a few seconds. "I had no idea. I don't know why ... well, I have some guesses, but it never occurred to me he wouldn't give the store to his kids—or at least just to Kathleen. They had their issues, but he loved his kids, you know?"

I patted his back. "Yeah, we know."

He continued, "Of course Detective Crowe asked if I knew about the will, and I think he and Frank both believed me when I said I didn't know, but there's no way I can prove John didn't tell me about it. Then they asked me to tell them anything I know about Kathleen and Paul that might help their case, as well as anyone else I thought might have anything against John, even if I didn't think they'd be capable of killing him. They said unless they could come up with a strong motive for anyone else, I was still the prime suspect and at some point soon they might have no choice but to arrest me."

Marty shook his head in disbelief. "When I was at the station earlier today, I didn't tell them everything because I didn't want to speak badly about anyone. But since it's my future—my *freedom* —on the line, I told them everything tonight. Nancy didn't try to stop me, so I figured if my lawyer was okay with it, it wouldn't hurt."

"And that 'everything' you told them was what?" my mom prompted from the love seat across from us, where she sat with Cynthia.

He took a deep breath. "Paul stole from the store many times over the years and John finally banned him from the building and changed the locks. Also, Kathleen's husband was fired from his job last year and is still unemployed, and last week John told me Kathleen was in the process of filing for divorce. I told them about the Hugh Canby lawsuit, though that was so long ago, I can't imagine why Hugh would do anything about it now." He turned to look at me. "And please don't tell Trixie this, but I also told them Todd caught her uncle Jerry shoplifting one day last month when I was out on my lunch break. Todd made Jerry stay until I got back instead of calling the police. I didn't turn him in, since we got the stuff back, but I did tell John what happened. Later, John told me the two of them had a pretty heated discussion over the phone, but he didn't give me details."

"Why in the blazes would Jerry McCoy need to shoplift?" my dad asked. "That doesn't seem like him at all."

"You're right," Marty's dad confirmed. "And I can't imagine him ever hurting anyone, much less swinging an axe into their head."

Cynthia squeaked, and Henry gave her a sheepish look. "Sorry, kiddo. You sure you want to be here and hear all this?"

My cousin nodded earnestly. "Yes. I want to be a newspaper reporter like my sister. I need to be able to hear stuff like this and not get squeamish."

"There's nothing wrong with being squeamish." Mom patted her on the knee. "In fact, if you ever stop being squeamish about murder, there might be something wrong with *that*. But you might need to learn to hide it."

Cynthia nodded and picked at a thread on the mauve throw pillow she was hugging.

"There's more," Marty said. "About Jerry, that is. Todd told me his mom said Jerry spends a lot of time at The Blue Barn these days." Todd's mom was a waitress at the bar, so she was a reliable source. "He started going a few days a week after June was diagnosed with cancer, and since she passed away in November, Jerry's there almost every day after work, and sometimes on his lunch hour. The day he was shoplifting, I could smell liquor on his breath."

"So maybe he attacked John in a drunken rage?" Cynthia mused.

"Could be," I said. "Though I really hope not. And even if he and John were on the outs because of the shoplifting, is that enough to want to kill John and pin it on Marty? Unless there's something else we don't know about, I don't see him as a main suspect."

"Me, neither," Mom said. "But if it was someone local who had a bone to pick with John, it might've been a crime of opportunity, if they somehow saw him at the store and decided to confront him, and it turned into an impromptu attack. That could mean they didn't set out to frame Marty."

"There's one more thing." Marty cleared his throat and looked down at his lap. "I didn't want to tell the police, but when I got to the store today, the back door wasn't locked, and there were no signs anyone had broken in. The only people who have keys since the locks were changed are John, me, Todd, and Madge."

We sat in silence, waiting for him to continue. When I realized he was finished talking, his point hit me. "You surely don't think Todd or Madge ..."

Marty shook his head vigorously. "No. I don't. Todd is a good kid, and Madge is trustworthy. She told the police she double checked all the locks when she left after cleaning last night. John probably unlocked the door himself and didn't lock it behind him. But when Detective Crowe asked who had keys, I had to tell him."

"But what motive would Todd or Madge have?" Kyle asked. He was parked in a kitchen chair right up against the front door and had been surprisingly quiet throughout the conversation. He was taking his self-proclaimed role as protector seriously. Not that the killer would dare to approach the house with the amount of vehicles parked outside.

Marty shrugged. "Neither of them have one as far as I know."

I slapped my hands against my knees. "Then they're not suspects in my book." I reached over and squeezed Marty's hand. "Don't feel bad about telling the police that. They asked the question, and you couldn't lie to them."

"What about the guy who is unemployed and getting divorced?" Cynthia asked. "He might need money. That could be a motive, right?"

"You're catching on fast, Cyn." I smiled at my cousin, and she beamed back at me. "That's John's son-in-law. And yes, if he doesn't have a job, and they're about to get divorced, both he and Kathleen are probably in dire need of cash. That makes them both suspects."

Brrrring!

I quickly stood and headed into the kitchen to answer the phone.

"Hello?"

"Hey," a deep voice said. Interestingly, it didn't cause flutters like it had earlier in the day.

"Mitchell, what's going on? Do you need something?"

"Do I need a reason to call you?" he teased.

I pressed my lips together and breathed in deeply through my nose before answering, "Yeah, you kinda do."

"Ah. Right. Anyway, is Marty there?"

My eyes narrowed. "Why?"

"I have a question for him."

"No, you don't get to ask him any more questions today. Plus, you should be talking to his lawyer, not him."

"Beckett ..."

"What's the question?" I demanded.

"The question isn't for you, and it's not directly about the case."

"Well, then it's not getting answered." I wasn't sure why I was being so stubborn about this.

"Beckett, let me talk to him." This request didn't come from the man on the other end of the line.

Chapter Seven

I turned, and Marty was standing a few feet from me, motioning for me to hand over the phone. I reluctantly passed it to him, but I didn't move away.

"This is Marty," he said into the handset.

I leaned toward him, trying to listen in, but Marty took a step back. I could hear Mitchell's voice, but not well enough to make out what he was saying. When I took another step toward Marty, he stepped back again.

"Uh-huh," he said. We each took yet another step, but he would soon run out of cord. "Yep. I'll make sure of it."

After another step, he was as far as he could go, but unfortunately that coincided with him saying goodbye. He handed me the phone, and I put it to my ear, only to hear the dial tone.

As I hung it up, I asked, "What was his question?"

He sighed and crossed his arms over his chest. "You're not going to like it."

"Try me."

"He asked if I'd make sure you stay at your parents' house until the killer is caught."

"What?" I sputtered. "Why couldn't he tell me that himself?"

One of Marty's eyebrows raised. "Would you have agreed?"

"No." My hands went to my hips. "He's not the boss of me."

"Well, I'm not the boss of you, either, but I'm asking you to please not stay here alone." His hands fisted at his sides. "I don't want to worry about you on top of everything else."

My heart went out to him, and I did what I'd wanted to do since he walked in the door earlier and wrapped my arms around him. He held me close and whispered into my hair, "Please do this for me."

"Okay. But I don't want to stay at my parents' house, because I don't want to put them and Cynthia in any danger by me being there."

"I'll stay here with you," Kyle said from the doorway.

We both turned to look at him as we let go of each other.

"If that's okay with you," Kyle added. He looked back and forth between Marty and me, letting us know he was talking to both of us.

"That's fine," I said before looking back at Marty. "But that means you'll be alone at your house."

"I'll be fine," he said. "You stay here with Kyle."

Marty's dad appeared in the doorway behind Kyle and said, "Son, if you were intentionally framed for the murder, you'll be fine. The killer will want you to be alive and the prime suspect. But what if you weren't framed, and the killer somehow sees you as a threat? I don't want you staying alone either."

My dad's head popped up behind the other guys. "Why don't you both stay at Henry's house?"

"But that might put Henry in danger," I argued.

"I don't care," Henry said.

"I care," Marty retorted.

My mom's voice ordered from the living room, "Everybody get back in here and let's figure this out together."

We all headed back to our seats.

"I don't want to put anyone in danger who isn't already," Marty said. "So I'll stay here with Beckett."

I sucked in a breath at the thought of the two of us staying here together with nobody else in the house. Not that I thought Marty would try anything, but at the same time, I kind of wanted him to try something. But with our lives potentially in danger, this was not the time to be thinking those thoughts.

"I'm staying, too," Kyle said. "If both of our trucks are parked outside, nobody's going to mess with Beckett. But I'll go home and get my gun, just to be safe."

"No," I said. "No guns."

"*Yes* guns," my mom said. "Unless you want me to stay here, too."

I groaned. "Come on, guys. Is this all really necessary?"

"Yes!" everyone else in the room cried out in unison.

"All right, fine. Marty and Kyle can both stay here. We have enough beds for everyone."

"Oh, I'm sleeping on the couch," Kyle said. "They'll have to get through me to get upstairs to either of you." He pointed back and forth between Marty and me.

"Hold on," Cynthia said, and we all turned to look at her.

"Yes?" I said.

"This doesn't have anything to do with who's staying where, but if Mitchell asked Marty to help keep Beckett safe from the killer, that means he's certain Marty isn't the killer." She looked around the room at each of us. "Right?"

That thought hadn't occurred to me, and she was probably right, but she didn't have all the facts. What she didn't know was that Mitchell also knew Marty was zero threat to me. He knew that if he couldn't be here to protect me, Marty was the next best option, other than my dad. He also knew I'd give in to Marty on the matter of me not being alone. The situation wasn't as cut-and-dried as she thought.

"Seems logical to me," Dad said. He was also clueless about the situation between Marty and me.

Cynthia added, "And you should probably call Mitchell and tell him where everyone will be tonight, once you know for sure, in case he needs to get in touch with any of you, and so maybe the police can keep an eye on the house."

"You're right," I said. "I'll call the station in a little bit."

"So are we set then?" Mom asked. "Marty and Kyle will stay here?"

Everyone nodded their heads.

Kyle stood and moved his chair away from the door. "Good. I'm gonna run home and get my gun and pack a bag." He looked at Marty. "Want me to grab stuff for you, too?"

"Yeah. Thanks, man."

Marty stood to shake Kyle's hand, but Kyle pulled him into a hug.

"Any time," Kyle said with a hard pat on Marty's back.

The others soon said their goodbyes and headed out, leaving Marty and me alone. He sat back down on the couch and patted the spot next to him. I collapsed into it, and he curled his arm around me.

"Is this okay?" he asked.

I cuddled into his side and put my head on his shoulder. "It's great."

We sat in silence for several minutes while he lightly stroked my arm with his callused fingers. It felt so right—so natural—to be snuggled up to him and just be quiet in each other's presence. My chest hurt as I thought about how he might be arrested for a murder he didn't commit, and we might never get to do this again. Tears formed in my eyes, and I willed them to stay put. Marty didn't need the stress of dealing with a crying woman.

Then he said, "Thanks for everything you did for me today."

"You're welcome. I'd do it every day if I needed to."

He kissed the top of my head where it rested on my shoulder, and goosebumps traveled from that spot all the way down to my toes.

"I know you would," he said.

I truly wanted to be there for this man every day. If there was anything today had taught me—as well as the past year—it was that excitement wasn't all it was cracked up to be. At least external excitement, that is. We'd experienced plenty of it over the past fourteen hours, and I'd have preferred not to go through any of it. Internal excitement was another thing, though, and I'd been feeling it every time I looked at or touched Marty today. I was feeling it now.

At the same time, I was irritated more than anything else when I talked to Mitchell. Sure, when I first saw him in the morning, there was some excitement, but it dwindled throughout the day—even now, when I was fairly certain he was determined not to arrest Marty for something he didn't do. Mitchell cared about me. He maybe truly loved me, as he claimed. But my feelings for him didn't come close to matching his for me. They also didn't match my feelings for the man I was cuddled up against.

To top it all off, once again, my family and friends had rallied around and were supporting me beyond anything I could ask for. I wouldn't have that somewhere else. I could maybe build up to it over time in another town with new people, but that could take decades. Cherry Hill was where I wanted to be—where I needed to be.

Did all that mean Marty was the man for me? Aunt Star had warned me not to simply pick one man or the other but to consider whether I wanted to be with either of them. I cared deeply for Marty. I didn't doubt that. In fact, I loved him. But did I love him the way a wife should love a husband? I thought maybe I did, but today was a strange day. I'd experienced so many emotions, I wasn't sure what was real and what was merely a byproduct of the prospect of Marty going to jail for something he didn't do.

Was this the time to tell Marty I wanted to date him? He probably needed to hear it, but I also didn't want Mitchell to get wind of it before he got Marty cleared. I didn't want my rejection of him to potentially cloud his thinking or judgment when it came to Marty.

The doorbell interrupted my thoughts before I could make a

full decision on what to tell Marty, if anything. I sat up so Marty could get up and let Kyle in.

Only it wasn't Kyle.

Officer Olivia Pierce stood on the other side of the glass storm door. I leapt to my feet and raced over. Had she come to arrest Marty?

I opened the storm door to let her in out of the cold. "What can we help you with, Olivia?" I asked, since Marty hadn't said a word.

"I was patrolling the area," she said. "Detective Crowe ordered me to specifically keep an eye on your house, your parents' house, and Marty's house. But there weren't any vehicles at Marty's house the last time I drove by, and I saw his truck was here, and, well ..." She seemed reluctant to finish her statement.

"And you wondered if he was staying here tonight?" I asked.

"Yeah. That."

"I am," Marty said, "and so is Kyle Korte, so we can make sure Beckett is safe. Kyle just headed home for a few minutes to grab a bag for each of us."

I noticed Marty didn't mention Kyle was also getting his gun, which was probably a smart idea.

Olivia cleared her throat, and I thought I detected a hint of a blush, which was odd.

"Good," she said. "That makes my job easier, and Detective Crowe will be glad to hear you won't be on your own tonight." She directed that last part at me.

"I was going to call and tell him," I said, "but I hadn't gotten around to it. Can you let him know?"

"Will do."

As we were speaking to Olivia, I watched Kyle's truck pull into the driveway. He grabbed two duffel bags out of the truck bed before making his way inside the house.

"Hello, Olivia," he said with a genuine smile—not his usual flirty smirk.

Much to my surprise, Olivia's face turned beet red. "Uh, hi,

Kyle." Her eyes slowly dragged down his body before she quickly turned and opened the storm door while saying over her shoulder, "I'll radio the station now and let them know you'll all be here tonight. And I'll drive by throughout the night to keep an eye on things."

"Sounds great," Kyle said. "You have a good night, Olivia."

"Y-yeah, you have a good one, too."

She scurried off to her patrol car, which was parked at the curb.

Marty crossed his arms over his chest and said to Kyle, "That was interesting."

"It sure was," I said. "I mean, we're used to seeing women run away from you, Kyle, but she seemed more pleased than annoyed by your presence before she hightailed it out of here."

"Hey!" Kyle said with a frown. "That's not nice." Then the corners of his mouth turned up. "But do you think she might be into me for real?"

Marty laughed. "As much as it pains me to admit it, yes. She's into you." He clapped a hand on his friend's shoulder. "You'd better snap her up before she changes her mind."

Kyle narrowed his eyes and pointed a finger at Marty. "Again, not nice. But I'll take it under advisement."

"Consider the hall bathroom to be yours," I said to Marty, "and I'll use the one in Aunt Star's room."

We stood facing each other in the guest room, where he'd be spending the night. I wasn't sure how to say goodnight to him. He didn't appear to know, either, as he stood with his hands in his jeans pockets, looking uncomfortable.

"Thanks for letting me stay here," he said.

"Are you kidding?" I replied. "Thank *you* for staying here. I could've handled being here on my own, but having you and Kyle in the house makes me feel perfectly safe. If you weren't here, every tiny noise would probably keep me awake, but now I can rest easy. I hope you can, too."

Marty held his left hand out toward me with his palm up, and I placed my right hand in it. He then pulled me to him and cocooned me in his arms. I melted into him and wrapped my arms around his waist, my body highly aware of all the places we were touching.

He said, "Thanks to Kyle downstairs playing bodyguard, and you snoozing safely in the room next door, I think maybe I'll be able to sleep. I just have to not think about *why* I'm staying at your house. I wish it were for happier reasons."

His big hands swept up and down my back, and my knees buckled. One of his hands went to my hip to steady me.

"You okay?" Marty murmured into my hair.

"Yeah, I'm just exhausted." Though that wasn't why my legs weren't working, my statement was true, which was one of the reasons we weren't going to have a conversation about us at the moment.

I peeked up at him, and when his gaze zeroed in on my mouth, I knew I needed to get out of the room quickly before we made this situation even more complicated than it already was. I'd never wanted to kiss anyone as badly as I wanted to press my mouth to his in that moment. Yet I went up on my tiptoes, gave him a light peck on the cheek, and took a step back. He reluctantly let me go.

"Good night," I said as I headed toward the door, my heart protesting my every step.

"Night, Beckett," he replied. "Sleep tight."

Chapter Eight

I awoke to heavy footsteps in the hall outside my room, and my heart momentarily leapt into my throat until I remembered Marty and Kyle were in my house. A glance at my alarm clock revealed it was 6:15, and I groaned. This was my second day in a row of waking up early, and my body didn't like it one bit. But I needed to get up and check on the guys and then do my best to solve the murder.

I threw my fluffy green robe on over my pajamas and grabbed some black stirrup pants and the long turquoise Liz Claiborne sweater I bought last week at Capital Mall. Then I headed down the hall to get ready in Aunt Star's bathroom.

Fifteen minutes later, I traipsed down the stairs, following the scent of coffee and bacon and the sound of Kyle singing "I Want to Know What Love Is" at the top of his lungs, nearly drowning out Foreigner singing it on the radio. I smiled at the sight of my friend standing at the stove sporting my pink and purple paisley apron over his Levi's 501s and plaid button-up shirt. His hips swayed to the beat of the music as he flipped the bacon and then grinned at me over his shoulder.

"Hope you don't mind I made myself at home in your

kitchen," he said and then reached over to push down the bread that was standing ready in the toaster.

"Mind that a man is barefoot in my kitchen making me breakfast?" I giggled. "Never!"

"Have a seat," Kyle said, pointing the spatula at the table. "I'm serving you as well. Coffee?"

I sighed as I sank down into my chair. "Yes, please." I usually started my day with Diet Coke, but that was often because it was quicker and easier than brewing coffee.

Kyle poured me a cup of coffee and set the sugar and creamer on the table next to me.

After taking a long sip, I asked, "Have you talked to Marty yet?" The shower was running in the upstairs hall bathroom when I headed down a minute ago, but I didn't know if he came downstairs earlier.

"He ran down to grab a cup of coffee and then headed right back up. He's not much of a morning person," Kyle shot me a wink, "for future reference."

I ignored his insinuation. He wasn't going to be the first person to hear my thoughts about my potential future with Marty.

Instead, I said, "So Olivia, huh? Have you spent any time with her?"

Kyle plated us each some bacon, scrambled eggs, and buttered toast and set the plates on the table before answering. "She goes to my church."

I wasn't aware Kyle was in the habit of going to church, but I knew his parents went to the Methodist church here in town.

"Oh, yeah?" I prompted.

He piled his bacon and eggs on one piece of toast, topped it with the other piece, and took a giant bite of his breakfast sandwich before continuing. "Yeah, after everything that's happened this past year, I thought maybe church might be good for me, so I started going again in the fall. I was right, and it's been even better since Olivia moved to town a couple months ago."

"She seems pretty shy," I said, "at least outside of doing her job. She's a good officer, from what I've seen and heard from Darren."

"She's real quiet," he replied, "but she's in the choir, and boy, can that woman sing!"

A dopey grin spread across his face, and I couldn't help but smile at him.

"So what have you done about it?" I asked.

"Well, I tried my usual flirting, but that doesn't work on her. She just blushes and doesn't respond and then leaves my presence as soon as possible. I've been trying to be less forward with her, but if last night was any indication, it might take some time for her to be comfortable around me."

I pat his hand. "Just be patient. It was obvious she was into you, but it was also obvious she didn't know what to do about it."

He nodded. "She's pretty young, though." His brow creased. "Do you think she's *too* young?"

I knew what he was getting at with that question. A few years earlier, Kyle was engaged to a younger woman, who called things off not too soon before the wedding was supposed to take place. She truly was too young—nineteen to his twenty-five. Though he'd gone back to his usual flirtatious self after that, he hadn't dated anyone seriously since then. Marty and I both thought he still had a thing for Marty's sister Karla. But she was married—albeit unhappily—so I was glad he seemed to be moving on.

"She's twenty-two and you're twenty-nine," I said. "You're both fully grown adults, so don't think too much about the age difference. And she seems like a great person." Unlike Karla or his ex-fiancée, I thought but didn't say.

"Yeah, she is. Anyway, I need to stop thinking about her and start thinking about how to get the police off Marty's back."

"Indeed," I said before popping a piece of bacon into my mouth.

Footsteps thundered down the stairs, and Marty soon walked

into the kitchen. My breath caught in my throat at the sight of him. His dark hair was still damp, and his button-up, hunter green flannel shirt clung to the planes of his chest just right. My gaze trailed down his light-wash jeans to his bare feet. I swallowed heavily and nearly choked on my bacon.

Marty rushed over and patted me on the back. "You okay?"

"Y-yes," I stuttered as my eyes watered. I was now enveloped in the scent of his aftershave, which set my heart racing even more than it already was.

I glanced over at Kyle, who merely smirked at me. He shook his head and laughed silently. I narrowed my eyes at him and sent him a silent order to stop it. In response, he pressed his lips together, but his eyes were still dancing.

Finally, Kyle pointed at the napkin-covered plate on the counter and said, "Your breakfast, my lord. Might need to pop it in the microwave for a few seconds."

I couldn't see Marty, since he was behind me, but I had no doubt he rolled his eyes at the "my lord" comment before grabbing the plate, sitting down, and starting to eat without reheating it.

Kyle linked his fingers behind his head and tilted his chair onto its back legs. "The good news is I didn't have to use my gun overnight, and you," he pointed his chin at Marty, "aren't in jail."

Marty and I both looked at Kyle and didn't say anything, waiting for him to continue.

"What?" he asked, spreading his arms wide.

"Usually," I said, "when someone says, 'the good news is,' that's followed up by what the bad news is. So what's the bad news?" My chest constricted at the thought there might be more bad news.

"There is no bad news." He shrugged. "I was just saying."

I said in exasperation, "The bad news is that as far as we know, Marty is still the main suspect. We need to change that."

"I have an hour or so before I need to be at work. What can I do?" Kyle asked before letting his chair drop back onto all four legs and focusing on Marty. "Speaking of work, what's happening with the store? Is it still a crime scene? Can you open today? Do you *want* to open today?"

Marty shook his head and then took a gulp of coffee before responding. "It's still a crime scene as far as I know. But I wouldn't open today anyway, out of respect for John and his family."

"Even though someone in John's family might be the reason he's dead?" Kyle asked.

"Even though," Marty replied. "It's the right thing to do."

My heart melted, and even with Kyle watching, I reached over and covered Marty's hand with my own. "You're a good man, Marty James."

His cheeks pinked up a little, and he didn't respond, but he gave me a small smile.

I asked, "Do you need to call Todd and anyone else who was scheduled to work today?"

Marty looked at the clock on the kitchen wall, which read 6:45. "I do. I wanted to wait until everybody might be awake, but I guess I should go ahead and call."

"If you want some privacy," I said, "you can use the phone in my room." I hadn't made my bed, but I was pretty sure all my dresser drawers were closed, so he wouldn't see anything embarrassing.

"I can do it here in the kitchen, but thanks."

While Marty made his calls, Kyle and I cleaned up the breakfast dishes and then moved into the living room, where Kyle had already folded up the bedding I gave him the night before. He'd even taken the pillowcase off the pillow.

He picked everything up. "Where's your laundry room?"

"Oh, you don't have to do that," I said. "I can take care of it."

"No need," he said. "Point me in the right direction."

"It's in the basement. Thanks."

Kyle headed downstairs, and I expected him to come right back up, but he didn't. A minute later, I could hear water running through the pipes, signaling he'd started the washing machine.

Marty entered the room before Kyle reappeared.

"Who knew Kyle Korte was such a domestic man?" I asked.

He raised his hand and took a seat on the couch next to me. "My house has never been so clean and organized as it's been since he moved in, and he's an excellent cook. He'll make a great house-husband someday."

"You better believe I will," Kyle said as he sauntered back into the room. "My mama taught me right. There's no such thing as women's work and men's work around the house. Everybody helps out with everything. Just call me a modern man." He plopped down sideways on one end of the loveseat and propped his socked feet up on the opposite arm, crossing them at the ankles. "Now tell me what you need me to do before I head off to work, and even once I get there. I could make calls or something in my downtime." Kyle worked at the local fertilizer plant, and business was slow in the winter.

"Why don't you head to The Check for a cup of coffee and see if anyone there knows anything helpful." I glanced at Marty. "Unless you have a better idea?"

"No, that sounds like a good plan."

I added, "And maybe stop for gas at McCoy's on the way. Chat with Jerry and Marvin for a minute." Marvin McCoy was Trixie's dad and Jerry's brother. The two men owned the gas station together.

"Beckett," Marty warned, "I don't think Jerry had anything to do with it."

"Maybe not," I said. *"Hopefully* not. But the gas station is only a hundred feet or so from the hardware store. Jerry or Marvin might've been there late Wednesday night or early yesterday morning. Maybe one of them saw something suspicious."

"Good point," Kyle said as he sat up and pulled on his work boots. "I'll see what I can find out. You gonna be here for a while, so I can call and fill you in on anything I learn?"

I looked at Marty, and he shrugged.

"I don't know yet," I said. "But if we're not here, you can leave a message on the answering machine. Also, tell Callie anything you learn before you leave The Check. And tell her everything else we've discovered. She might be able to tell you if we're off base on anything or if we've missed something important."

Kyle saluted me before heading to the door. "Be safe, you two."

"We will," Marty said. "Thanks for staying here last night. Appreciate it more than you know."

"I'd do it again in a heartbeat. In fact, I'll do it again tonight if needed."

"We'll keep you posted," I said. "Thanks, Kyle."

When the door closed behind him, Marty's head fell back against the couch.

"What are we going to do?" he asked.

"What do you want to do?"

He angled his head toward me. "Go back to sleep and pretend none of this happened." I watched his Adam's apple bob as he swallowed. "I can't believe John is gone."

I kept forgetting that not only was Marty a suspect in a murder he didn't commit, but he'd also lost his long-time boss and good friend. I took his hand and held it tightly, and he squeezed back.

He said, "I can't even call his kids and tell them I'm sorry, because they probably think I did it, or maybe *they* did it."

"I wish this wasn't such a mess." I scooted right up next to him and leaned my head against his shoulder.

"Me, too," he whispered. After a few moments of silence, he said, "You don't have to work today, right?"

The church office was closed on Fridays, since we all worked Sunday mornings and Wednesday evenings. "No, which means I can run around town and find out who really killed John."

"I still have mixed feelings about that," Marty admitted.

"About me working on this case?"

"Yeah." He squeezed my hand again. "I mean, I want someone else to be arrested—the real killer. And I know you're good at doing this kind of thing. But I also don't want you to put yourself in danger for me."

"Nobody's going to hurt me in broad daylight," I stated confidently.

"Uh, do you remember what happened at my house last summer? And at Jacqui's house in the fall? Both of those were during the day."

"I do remember. And I also recall not getting hurt either time."

Marty sighed heavily. "You were lucky."

"I like to call it divine intervention."

"Call it whatever you want, but I don't like it. I don't want you to get hurt."

"And I don't want you to go to jail. Which is more important?"

"You're more important."

I sat up straight and turned to face him. "I'm not. Neither of us is more important than the other. But I'm not going to let you go to jail, Marty. I'm not. And if that means potentially putting myself in danger in the process, then so be it."

Brrrring!

Chapter Nine

"Everything okay over there?" Mitchell said from the other end of the line. I felt a bit nauseous at the sound of his voice. I wasn't sure whether it was because I was excited about him being back in town, because I'd been spending quality time with another man, or because I was worried he was calling to tell me they were arresting Marty.

"All good," I said. "We had an uneventful night." I didn't consider spending time cuddled up on the couch with Marty to be uneventful, but that was the last thing Mitchell would want to know about.

"Glad to hear it. Are Marty and Kyle still there?"

"Kyle just left to grab breakfast at The Check." I left out the part about him fishing for information while he's there. "Marty is still here, and I don't know what his plans are."

"Okay. Will you please make sure you don't go anywhere alone until the killer's caught?"

I rolled my eyes but agreed. "Yes. I mean, I might drive places by myself, but I'll make sure I'm not alone once I get to where I'm going."

"Thank you."

"You're welcome. Are you just checking in, or do you need to talk to Marty?" I propped a hip against the kitchen counter.

"Both. Are you going to hassle me about talking to him? I got approval from Nancy to call him, just so you know."

I sighed. "I'll allow it as long as *you* don't hassle *him.*"

"Not planning on it."

"Good. I'll get him."

Mitchell quickly said, "Hang on a sec."

"Yeah?" I replied.

I heard footsteps and when I turned, Marty was leaning against the doorway from the living room into the kitchen. His thumbs were in his belt loops, and he raised his eyebrows at me. I held up a finger to let him know I wasn't finished on the phone. Then I let my gaze wander down his body once again.

Mitchell asked, "What do you know about Todd at the hardware store?"

It took me a few seconds to register his question. "Todd?" I said this for Marty's benefit, so he'd know what we're talking about. "He's a good kid. I can't imagine any scenario in which he did this."

"That seems to be the general consensus around here, but I wanted to check with you because I knew you'd be honest."

My eyebrows raised. "And nobody else would?"

"I'm not saying that. Just that if anyone had slight reservations, they probably wouldn't say them to me because of the potential ramifications. But I knew you'd give it to me straight. What about Jerry McCoy? I know he's Trixie's uncle, but what are your thoughts on him? Could you see him doing it?"

"Not the Jerry I know, but from what I've heard, he's changed lately. So even though I hate to say it, I can't be sure about him anymore."

Marty's eyes looked sad when I said that, but he knew I was right.

Mitchell said, "Okay, thanks. One more person I'd like to get your opinion on: Donnie Masters."

"Donnie? You think he had something to do with this?"

Marty's eyes went as wide as mine.

"We're just looking into some things," Mitchell said. "That's all I can say. So what do you know about him?"

"I don't really know him, so I guess I don't have an opinion. I don't think many people love him, but that's par for the course for a lot of lawyers, isn't it?"

"I guess. I'm ready to talk to Marty now, unless there's anything you need to tell me."

"Just that he didn't do it."

Mitchell sighed. "I know he didn't. But we still don't have any compelling evidence against anyone else. We need to find something, and fast. Paul has gotten a lawyer, and he'll soon be putting pressure on us to arrest Marty. There's enough evidence to do so."

"Well, get out there and find evidence against someone else!"

"I'm trying, Beckett. We're all trying. I wish Darren was here." I was surprised to hear him admit that. The two got along fine, and they highly respected each other's skills, but they both liked to be in charge. "We could really use his help on this one."

"Are you going to try to get in touch with him?" I asked.

"No. Olivia called Princess Cruises, and they said based on the ship's location, they wouldn't be able to get home much faster than their current plans, so there's really no reason to bother him and Starla."

I sighed. "Yeah, I was thinking the same. Hey, hold on a minute. When we went to see Donnie yesterday, he let it be known in a roundabout way that Marty was named in the will, but he didn't come right out and say it. Is that helpful at all? I thought it was kind of weird he said anything, because of confidentiality and all. But maybe he knew Marty would want a reason why he couldn't represent him."

"Wait. You and Marty met with Donnie?"

"Yes. After Marty talked to you at the station the first time, we realized he needed a lawyer, and we went to Donnie. He said he was the executor of the will and therefore couldn't represent Marty because it would be a conflict of interest. When we questioned him further, he said the estate mattered to Marty."

"Did Marty know Donnie was John's lawyer?"

"Yeah, that's why we went to him first." I paused. "That proves Marty didn't know what was in the will, doesn't it? Because if he knew, he would've known to pick a different lawyer."

"Well, it's not technically proof, but what you're saying is logical."

"Hold on yet another minute," I said. "Donnie knew what was in the will. He's the only person that you can prove knew what was in it." I nodded at my own conclusion. "That's why you want to know about him. He's the one person you could definitely say had the knowledge to frame Marty."

Surprisingly, Mitchell chuckled. "I don't know why I try to keep things from you. You just figure everything out anyway."

"Yep. And the more I know, the quicker we can find the real killer. So, is there anything else you need to tell me? What about people's alibis? I don't want to waste my time tracking down information on somebody you've already cleared."

He sighed. "Fine. I'll tell you. But don't be spreading it around that you heard this from me."

"I wouldn't dream of it."

I motioned Marty over to the table, where we pulled two chairs right up next to each other. I held the phone a couple inches away from my ear so he could also hear. He leaned in toward me, and I tried not to think about how close our mouths were to each other.

Mitchell began, "Kathleen and her husband are living separately at the moment. She claims she was home with the kids at the time of the murder. We can't corroborate that, but the kids are young enough that it's hard to believe she'd leave them alone for seven-plus hours while she drove up here, lured her dad to the store, did the deed, and then drove back home in time to answer the phone when we called. We can't completely rule her out, but she's not our main focus right now."

Marty exhaled deeply. He was relieved it probably wasn't Kathleen, as was I. I didn't know her well, but I liked her, and I knew Marty did, too.

"Does her husband have an alibi?" I asked.

"He's in Dallas visiting his parents. Frank talked to him on the phone at their house, so we know he's there, which means he couldn't have done it."

"Okay. What about Paul and his wife?"

Mitchell said, "We can't prove where either of them were overnight Wednesday. They both say they were at home, but in a murder investigation, I'm not inclined to trust a spouse to tell the truth. Plus, when Jake called their house around 7:15 a.m., Janis answered, and she said Paul had just left for work. However, the store he works at doesn't open until nine. Nobody answered the phone there until after that. He was there then, but his boss couldn't verify he was there early, so he's unaccounted for before 9:00."

"Interesting."

"Isn't it? All right, that's all you're getting from me this morning. Can I talk to Marty now?"

I moved the phone closer to Marty, but he didn't take it from me. I took that as my cue to listen in.

"This is Marty," he said into the phone.

"Were you hoping to open the store today, once we're able to declare it's no longer a crime scene?" Mitchell asked.

"No. We'll stay closed today and tomorrow out of respect for John and his family."

"Okay. Do you think you could meet me over there in an hour or two? I want you to take a look around and see if anything seems to be out of place. If you were planning to open, we'd do it now, so we could go ahead and clear the scene, but I've got something else I'd like to take care of first. Nancy said it was fine for you to do this, and she'll be there, too."

"Yeah, I can do that. You might want to ask Todd to come, too, and Madge. Todd closed the store on Wednesday, and then Madge was there cleaning after that. So they've been there since I have. Well, other than ..."

"Yeah. Gotcha. Would you mind calling them? That'll save me some time, which means we can get this all done sooner."

"Will do."

"Thanks. I'll see you over there around 8:30."

They said their goodbyes, and Marty hung up the phone. Then he called Todd and Madge, who both said they could meet him and Mitchell at the store. He rejoined me at the table when he was done.

"What motive would Donnie have for killing John?" Marty asked.

"I have no earthly idea." I tapped my fingers on the table. "But since Mitchell is looking into him, he must have one." Something niggled in my mind. "Hold on. Did you say Donnie plays poker with your dad?"

Marty nodded slowly. "Yeah. Why?"

"I realize most people who regularly play poker with their friends don't have a gambling problem, but what if Donnie does? Or what if he's in financial trouble? Do you think your dad would know?"

He tilted his head to the side. "Maybe. We can ask him."

"Okay, we'll call him in a minute, but this might be a silly lead to chase. I'm not sure how killing John would get Donnie any money."

"Yeah, but we might as well look into it. Let me call Dad."

Marty got up to grab the phone again and dialed Henry. Again, we both listened in on the conversation.

When Marty asked about Donnie's financial situation, his dad said, "I don't know anything for certain, but he keeps trying to up the value of the chips at poker. None of the rest of us have any interest in doing that, though. We play for fun and bragging rights. There's not a whole lot of money involved, and the rest of us like it that way because our wives would kill us if we lost more than ten bucks each time. He also seems to be more upset when he loses than he used to, even though you'd think the amount of money at stake would be pocket change for a lawyer."

"Has he ever been to Las Vegas?" I asked before realizing Henry didn't know I was listening in.

"Oh. Hello, there, Becky." Henry sounded pleased to hear my voice, which was a relief. "Come to think of it, yes. He and Wanda went to Vegas for New Year's."

Marty's eyes met mine. This was all information we needed to pass along to the police.

"All right. Thanks, Dad," Marty said before ending the call.

"You gonna tell Mitchell all of that?" I asked him.

He turned slightly toward me and rested his arm on the back of my chair. "Of course. Or you can. I'd like you to go to the store with me, if you're up for it. You might see something the rest of us don't."

"But I don't spend much time in the store." In fact, I hadn't been there in months, since I'd been avoiding Marty.

"I know, but you're really observant. I'd like you to come, if that's okay."

"Sure. And then I might actually go into the church office for a little while even though I'm off work today, if I can find someone to be there with me. Based on experience, I think some people might call there to give me information that might help with the case." I imagined nearly everyone in town would be doing everything they could to help solve the murder and get Marty cleared. "Plus, I can keep an eye on the hardware store through the window by my desk and see if anybody stops by there looking suspicious. What are you planning to do until you head to the store?"

"Is it okay if I stay here?" he asked. "I don't want to go home, where people might call or even try to visit me. If anyone has information they think might be helpful, they'll call you. Anyone who would call me or come to my house would want to know how I am, and I honestly don't feel like talking about it."

My chest tightened. "Not even with me?"

"Of course I want to talk to you. But not random people."

I smirked. "Glad to know I'm not random people."

His hand moved from the back of my chair and swept under my hair until it rested on the nape of my neck. It was all I could do to keep my body from shuddering at the intimate contact.

"You're most certainly not," he said in a low voice as his eyes searched mine.

Ding-dong!

I nearly jumped out of my chair at the sound of the doorbell. I couldn't decide if the interruption was a good or bad thing, but I was leaning toward bad.

Chapter Ten

"Kathleen," Marty said from my front doorway, with me peeking around his much bigger frame. He'd insisted on opening the door, and I didn't contradict him, but I also wanted to know who was there. John's daughter was the last person I expected.

I sucked in a gulp of air before reaching around Marty and opening the storm door enough so she could hear me. "What are you doing here?"

"I came here to see you," she said to me. "I didn't expect *you* to be here, too." This part was directed at Marty.

"Me?" I asked. "Why did you come to see me?"

"Dad told me how you helped solve the murders last year, and I hoped you could help with this one, too." She eyed Marty warily. "But this is probably not the best idea. Sorry to bother you."

Kathleen turned and started back down the front steps.

"Wait," Marty said as he opened the storm door the rest of the way.

Kathleen swiveled back around and looked up at us with a questioning gaze.

"I'm sorry about your dad," he said to her. "I loved him, and I didn't kill him. You might not believe me right now, but it's true."

Her shoulders sagged. "I believe you."

"And for what it's worth," Marty added, "I don't think you killed him, either."

"Thanks," she said with sad eyes.

Even though I still had some minor suspicions of Kathleen being the killer, I realized that if she wanted help finding the killer, then it probably wasn't her, unless she was trying to throw us off the scent. However, I wouldn't have any idea until I talked to her. I still might not know after that, but it was worth a shot.

I looked up at Marty and had a brief unspoken conversation with him. He gave me a slight nod, and I moved in front of him and said to Kathleen, "If you're still willing to talk with me, I can meet you at The Check in about ten minutes. Does that work for you?"

She looked back and forth between Marty and me a few times before responding, "Yeah, I can do that."

"Great," I said. "I'll see you then." I waved and then closed the door as she walked back to her car.

"You sure this is a good idea?" Marty asked.

I pursed my lips before saying, "I thought you believed she's not the killer."

"I'm ninety-five percent sure she's not. But the other five percent makes me a little nervous about you meeting with her."

"We'll be in public," I reminded him. "Kyle will probably still be there. I can also call my mom and see if she'll go as well. She can sit a few tables away and keep an eye on things."

"She's not working today?" Marty asked.

"No, she only works Tuesday through Thursday. She changed her schedule a few weeks ago so she can take long weekends to go to St. Louis and visit Rafe's family."

Marty's eyebrows raised. "Your brother lives in St. Louis now?"

I forgot I hadn't spoken to him since Christmas, which is

when I found out my brother's company was transferring him from their Chicago office to St. Louis. "Yeah, they just moved there. Aunt Star and I went to help them move in a couple weekends ago."

He smiled. "That's great. I know how much you love those kids."

I couldn't help smiling back at him. "Being an aunt is the best!" And my seven-year-old niece Jodie and three-year-old nephew Brandon were also the best. I was ecstatic I'd now get to see them much more often than in the past.

"Anyway," I said, "I'll call Mom real quick and ask her if she can head to The Check."

"What about your cousin?" Marty asked.

"Oh." I had completely forgotten about Cynthia. "She can go with Mom. They'll be perfectly safe at the diner."

"Tell me what I can do to help you," I said to Kathleen. We sat across from each other in a booth in the back corner of The Check. I sat where I could see the entire room, whereas she couldn't see anyone but me and the wall.

My mom and Cynthia sat a few booths away, along with Veronica, who I also called before heading over. She had readily agreed to hang out with me at the church later today. I wondered if Kathleen would notice Mom and comment on her presence, but she zeroed in on me as soon as she entered the diner. A few people expressed their condolences to her as she passed them on her way to my booth, but she simply said thanks and carried on without stopping to chat.

"If it's not too personal," she said after she greeted me, "I'd like to understand why Marty was at your house this morning."

Before I could answer, Callie appeared at our table. "Kathleen," she said, "I'm sorry about your dad. He was a good man."

Kathleen's eyes filled with tears. "He was. Thanks."

Callie patted her on the shoulder. "What can I get you? Coffee? Breakfast? Both?"

"I'll take some coffee, bacon, and scrambled eggs."

"Gotcha. And the usual for you?" Callie asked me.

"Yes, please." I'd already eaten breakfast, but The Check had the best blueberry pancakes in mid-Missouri, and I couldn't pass them up.

Callie quickly grabbed a coffee carafe and poured the steaming liquid into the coffee cup that already sat in front of Kathleen. "Food will be right up."

As she walked away, I said to John's daughter, "As for Marty, we're friends. We got to know each other pretty well after the murders last year. Last night, he and his roommate Kyle Korte spent the night at my house. They were concerned about my safety, since everyone knows I get involved in police business." I pointed to Kyle, who was sitting on a stool at the counter while chatting to the other waitress. "That's Kyle over there. He was in my class in school. Do you know him?"

Kathleen turned to look at Kyle before returning her focus to me. "He looks familiar, but you two are quite a bit younger than me, so I don't know him. Anyway, thanks for explaining about Marty. I really don't think he could've done this, even though the evidence points to him. Someone was obviously trying to frame him."

Callie slid a glass of Diet Coke in front of me before heading to the kitchen again.

I smiled at Kathleen's deduction. "I agree. Now, how can I help you?"

"Well, I don't know how this works," she said. "Do people just tell you things, and you put it all together to figure it out?"

I swallowed a mouthful of fizzy goodness and bobbed my head from side to side. "More or less. Let's start with who you think might have reason to hurt your dad in some way. Don't think of it as who might want to kill him, because you'll filter those answers by who you think could actually kill someone. In my experience, the people who commit violent crimes in a place like Cherry Hill aren't usually people you'd think would be capable of it."

"Okay. Well, you probably know about the lawsuit from a long time ago?" Kathleen asked.

I nodded in confirmation, and she continued, "I won't get into that, then. Dad also told me about Jerry McCoy shoplifting from the store, but since he didn't turn Jerry in, I don't think Jerry would have reason to hurt him."

"That's a great point." I tapped my fingernails on the table. "I knew about the shoplifting but hadn't considered that your dad letting him off the hook meant Jerry would be grateful to him, not upset with him."

"I guess maybe he could've been afraid Dad would tell other people or even the police later on, though," Kathleen mused.

"True. So he's not completely off the hook. Who else?" I prompted, wondering if she'd mention the problems between her dad and brother.

"A month or so ago, Dad told me he wasn't fully confident in Donnie Masters anymore—as his lawyer, I mean. He didn't say why, though." She paused for a minute and I could almost see the gears turning in her head as she thought about something. "I guess something must've happened between them when he went in to change the will."

"Did you know he changed the will?"

Kathleen shook her head vehemently. "No. I didn't. And I know you're going to ask if I'm upset about it, and the answer is yes. Not so much because I didn't get the store, but because I don't know why. I know why he didn't trust Paul anymore, especially when it came to the store, but not me." Tears filled her eyes. "What did I do to deserve that?"

"I don't know." Though I guessed it was at least partly because Marty had become like a son to her dad and had worked at the store for two decades. "And we'll probably never know." I patted her hand from across the table. "I'm so sorry you're having to deal with all this."

She sniffled. "Thanks. And in case you're wondering, he did leave most of the rest of his estate to me. He didn't leave anything to Paul."

"Really?" I asked. "How do you think Paul feels about that?"

Kathleen looked down at her hands. "He won't talk to me, but he's got to be mad, even though he should understand why Dad did it." She looked back up at me. "He hadn't talked to Dad in a long time. He's ... I shouldn't say this about my brother, but he's not a good man. I know Dad kept hoping he'd come around and change his ways, but ..." She didn't need to finish her sentence.

I took a deep breath and asked a question I didn't want to ask but needed to. "Do you think your brother would've been mad enough to kill your dad over the will—either because he thought he'd inherit a lot of money or because he knew your dad had changed it and was angry about that?"

Kathleen wouldn't meet my eyes when she whispered, "I don't know."

My heart went out to her. What would it be like to think your sibling might be capable of murdering your parent?

She continued, "But I'm not sure how Paul would've known Dad cut him completely out. I can't imagine Dad told him. It seems like nobody knew about the updated will other than Donnie."

I had a question about Donnie, but first I needed another answer. "If you don't mind me asking, you said most of the rest of the estate goes to you, but not all, so who gets the rest?"

"He left twenty-five thousand to the VFW. Dad served in Korea."

"Oh. I didn't know that." I wasn't old enough to remember the Korean War, but the VFW was involved in a lot of events around town, and they led the Fourth of July parade. I figured I would've seen John in his uniform at some point.

"Yeah, he didn't like to talk about the war, and I don't think he was very involved in the VFW. I'm surprised he left them some money—especially that much."

My body stiffened when my thoughts jumped back to last summer's parade. Donnie Masters was part of the VFW contingent.

"What?" Kathleen asked. "You look like you've had a revelation."

"Sorry but not sorry for butting in," Callie said as she slid our plates in front of us, "but I've heard some of what you've said." She lowered her voice so only we could hear. "Donnie is the treasurer of the local VFW."

Chapter Eleven

"Tell us what she said," Veronica demanded when I sat down across the booth from her.

Kathleen had left the diner, and I still had about ten minutes before I needed to head two doors down to the hardware store to meet up with Marty, Mitchell, and the others.

"Where's Mom?" I asked. "She'll want to hear this, too." Mom had left about ten minutes after I arrived, and I had no idea why.

"She went home to change her clothes and get ready for work," Cynthia explained from her seat next to me. "A woman named Aggie called as we were walking out the door. She said her baby was sick, and she asked if Aunt Minda could cover for her today. Your mom didn't want to take the time to get ready then, since you needed her here, but once she knew you were safe, she headed back home. She made me promise to stay with Mrs. Coker until she gets off work later."

My hand went to my chest. "Oh, poor little Adam. Did Aggie say what was wrong with him?" Aggie's baby boy was only a few weeks old. Mom wasn't happy that she was already back to work so soon, but as a single mom, Aggie didn't have much choice.

"A fever, was all she said."

"I hope he's okay," I said. "Maybe I'll stop by to check on them after I meet the guys at the hardware store."

"No," Veronica said. "Cynthia and I will go, and then we'll head to the church to meet you after that. You just keep doing everything you can to clear Marty's name. Now, tell us what we need to know."

"First, let's get Callie over here," I said. "I need to see if she has anything to add from what she's heard or what Kyle might have found out earlier."

I waved Callie over to us. She picked up the coffee carafe and filled cups as she made her way to our table. Most of the breakfast crowd had cleared out, so I hoped she'd be able to stick around for a few minutes to chat with us.

She sat down next to Veronica and said, "I'm guessing you want to know what I know, so here goes. Kyle stopped by McCoy's on his way here. Jerry wasn't there. Marvin told Kyle that Jerry called in sick today, so he didn't find out anything there. Marvin also said he wasn't at the station Wednesday night or early yesterday morning before the murder. But if you want my opinion, Jerry didn't do this. I'll tell you who you might want to look into, though, other than Donnie Masters," she shot a quick glance at Veronica before adding, "and that's Jacqui Storm."

My eyebrows shot up. "What? Why?"

I couldn't imagine how Jacqui had anything to do with this murder. She was Suzanne LaHaye's daughter and grew up in Cherry Hill, but she left town after high school and only moved back last year. She couldn't have had much contact with John during that time, if any.

Callie cut another look at Veronica and said, "Because Suzanne and John were dating."

Veronica lurched back in her seat. "What? That's preposterous!"

I was shocked, too, though I quickly realized it made sense. They were both widowed, and they had been friends their entire adult lives.

"It's not," Callie said. "She's been going to visit him in Springfield every week or two for the past few months." She braced herself before saying, "Sometimes she spends the night."

"You're lying!" Veronica exclaimed.

"I'm sorry, Mrs. Coker," Callie said to her, "but it's true."

Veronica's hand went to her throat. "Why wouldn't she tell me?"

"Maybe because she spends the night," Callie said in a matter-of-fact tone.

I glanced at the clock behind the counter. I needed to leave. "We can get into all that later," I said with a compassionate look at Veronica, "but I've gotta go, so for now, Callie, tell us what that has to do with us looking into Jacqui for John's murder."

Callie held up two fingers. "She has two potential motives, both related to the possibility of Suzanne and John getting married. One, a marriage would possibly take Suzanne away from Cherry Hill, which would mean Jacqui would lose her built-in babysitter. And two, you know how Jacqui's always hard up for money. She could've been afraid all of Suzanne's wealth would end up with John or his kids instead of her someday."

When I stepped out of The Check and turned down the sidewalk toward the hardware store, Mitchell was standing outside the front door chatting with Nancy, Todd, and Madge. As I approached them, Marty's pickup pulled into a parking spot a few yards down.

The three on the sidewalk greeted me, and Mitchell gave me a searching look. I gave him what I hoped was a neutral look in return. This wasn't the time to even think about our future, much less communicate anything about it, even silently. But who was I kidding? I was going to think about it. While I'd gotten much closer to Marty over the previous twenty-four hours and felt more comfortable with him than I could've imagined, my breath still caught when I first spotted Mitchell a few seconds earlier.

"Looks like we're all here," Marty said when he stepped up beside me.

Mitchell raised his eyebrow at me. "You're planning to go in, too? Why?"

I nodded, and Marty spoke before I could. "I asked her to come with us to see if anything seemed off to her. She's pretty observant. That okay with you, detective?" There was a slight edge to his voice that I'd never heard before.

I glanced between the men, hoping they weren't about to get into an argument about me in front of the others. Thankfully, they didn't.

Mitchell shrugged. "Sounds good. Always nice to have another set of eyes." He removed one end of the crime scene tape in front of the door and nodded to Marty. "I'll let you do the honors. I assume you have your key. Don't worry about touching the door. We've already checked it for prints." He then spoke to the rest of us. "But when we're inside, don't touch anything. If you see anything out of the ordinary, we might need to dust for more prints."

We all nodded as we trooped in after Marty and stopped in the entryway next to the check-out counter.

"I'll head back to turn on the lights," Marty said. "Wait here."

Mitchell cleared his throat. "I'll go with you."

Marty narrowed his eyes at Mitchell. "Don't trust me?"

"You're still a suspect." Mitchell spread his hands wide. "I gotta do it all by the book. It's as much for your protection as mine."

"All right. Come on, then."

The two men made their way through the dimly lit aisles, and soon the overhead fluorescent lights flickered on.

When they returned, Mitchell said, "I want to thank you all for doing this. I know it's hard, because you all cared for John, but this is important to help not only the case overall, but also to potentially uncover new evidence that could help Marty. Just so you know, we've cleaned up the blood, so you don't need to worry about seeing that. What I want you to do first is hang out right here and look around. Does anything look off? Is something out of place from where it usually is? Is anything missing? Can you see anything that isn't normally here?"

We all turned in slow circles, taking everything in—from the checkout counter to the shelving to the steps leading to the second floor.

"There!" Madge said as she took a step toward the stairs.

Mitchell lightly grasped her elbow to halt her progress. "Hold up. Don't touch anything. Stay right here and tell me what you see."

"Right there." She pointed toward the stairs. "See that round thing on the fourth step, right up against the edge on the right?"

We all craned our necks but I couldn't see what she was talking about.

"It's almost the same color as the stairs." She tugged Mitchell closer to the brown carpeted stairs. "I think maybe it's a button. See it?"

"Yes. Hold on." Mitchell took a camera out of his jacket pocket, approached the stairs, and took a photo of the object. Then he pulled out a pair of tweezers and a small evidence bag. He grabbed the item with the tweezers, inspected it closely before turning toward us, and then held the brown button out for us to look at. While it wasn't extra fancy, it also wasn't a run-of-the-mill button. The outside edge was beveled, and a wavy line circled the holes about halfway between them and the edge. Its size suggested it was from a button-up shirt—possibly a cuff.

"You sure this wasn't there when you cleaned Wednesday night?" he asked Madge.

She nodded. "I'm positive. I vacuum the stairs with the hose attachment, and I make sure to get into all the nooks and crannies. That would've been sucked right up if it was there when I cleaned."

D.A. Wilkerson

Mitchell then asked, "This button look familiar to any of you?"

I shook my head. "Not me, but I wouldn't think plain, dark brown is a common color for buttons, especially on a shirt. Most are white, clear, or tortoiseshell."

Nancy added, "I agree. And even though it has that wavy line, which is kind of feminine, I don't think it's from a woman's shirt, because I don't think I've ever owned a shirt with brown buttons. It seems more likely a man's shirt would have them."

"What makes you so sure this is from a shirt?" Mitchell asked.

"The size," Madge, Nancy, and I said in unison.

"Fair enough," he replied. "Guys, you have any thoughts to add on the button?"

Marty and Todd both said no, and Mitchell dropped the button into the evidence bag.

"All right, then," he said. "Let's keep looking."

"Wait a minute," I said. "If that button appeared between when Madge cleaned and now, then wouldn't that mean the killer went upstairs? Should we go up there and see what else might be out of place?"

"I was going to get to the second floor later," Mitchell said, "to see if Marty could see anything out of the ordinary in his office, but we might as well do it now since we've got a good reason to do so. Follow me, and again, don't touch anything—not even the railing."

Mitchell and Todd moved quickly up the stairs, with Madge and Nancy following closely behind. Marty held his elbow out to me and said in a low voice, "I know you're not the best with stairs, even with a railing, so you'd better hold onto me."

My cheeks pinked as I remembered tripping and falling near the top of these very stairs several months earlier, which resulted in me learning how Marty felt about me.

"Thanks." I grabbed onto his arm and we carefully made our way up.

As we ascended, I considered the fact that Marty immediately offered me assistance and Mitchell apparently didn't think about the fact I might need help due to my bad leg. True, Mitchell was focused on the job at hand, but Marty was just as focused on finding evidence to help himself out, yet he still thought about my needs.

When we got to the top and looked around, everyone agreed nothing seemed out of the ordinary with the shelves and items for sale on the second floor. Mitchell led us to the back and motioned for Marty to unlock the door to his office.

"We dusted this doorknob for prints yesterday, so don't worry about that," Mitchell said. "And for the record, the door was locked yesterday, so we didn't come in here."

Mitchell looked at me, Todd, and Madge. "You three can stay out here. Nancy, feel free to go in with Marty. Madge, do you clean the office, too?"

"No." She shook her head. "And I don't have a key."

"I clean the office when it needs cleaning," Marty explained to Mitchell. "Nobody has a key other than John and me. We changed this lock, too, after we had the problems with Paul."

"Okay," Mitchell replied. "Go on in and look around. If you need to open drawers or anything, put these on first." He pulled a pair of rubber gloves from his pocket and handed them to Marty.

The rest of us watched as Marty entered the small space and moved around behind the metal desk.

"Ah, shoot," he said as his shoulders slumped.

Chapter Twelve

"What is it?" Mitchell asked Marty. "Is something missing?"

"I can't answer that yet. This bottom drawer," he pointed at the desk, "is always kept locked, and I have the only key. But it's unlocked now. See how the key hole is turned sideways?"

Michell knelt down by the drawer in question. "Yes. It looks like it might've been picked. Were these scratches here before?"

Marty shook his head. "No."

"What do you keep in this drawer?" Mitchell asked as he pulled on a rubber glove and opened the drawer. "Can you tell if anything is missing?"

Marty peered down. "Not at first glance. This is where I keep the bank statements, employee files, and other important documents nobody else needs to see."

Marty put one of the rubber gloves on, sat in the chair with Mitchell's permission, and flipped through the file folders. "It doesn't look like anything is missing." He pointed to one. "But see how this top bank statement isn't square with the rest of them? I think somebody pulled it out, because I always tap them all back together before putting them into the folder."

"Great catch." Mitchell got back to his feet. "We'll head over to the bank after we leave here to make sure nobody made any unauthorized withdrawals yesterday." He pointed to the folder. "Okay if I take this? I'll make sure you get it back when we're finished."

Marty looked to Nancy, who nodded her assent.

"Take anything you think will help," Marty said.

"We'll dust the desk and files for prints, too," Mitchell said as he carefully pulled the folder out of the drawer, "though I doubt we'll find any other than yours. The killer obviously wore gloves, but there's a chance he or she took them off to go through the files more easily." He glanced at Marty. "If you want to give me the key to the drawer and office, I'll make sure we lock everything back up when we're done."

"What about the office door?" I gestured to the doorknob. "How did the killer unlock it? It doesn't have scratches like somebody picked the lock. Maybe they took John's keys after they killed him?"

Mitchell nodded. "I'll check in the evidence box for that key. The back door key was on John's keyring, but we didn't think to look for a different key for the office."

He then led us around the rest of the store, but nobody noticed anything else that seemed suspicious, so Todd and Madge went home, and Mitchell, Marty, and Nancy headed down the street to the bank. I didn't try to go with them, since I knew that would annoy Mitchell. Marty would tell me what happened later, and I could also ask my mom to fill me in since she was working at the bank.

I watched the two men walk down the sidewalk toward the bank together, and my heart squeezed. I was going to be breaking one of their hearts in the near future, and I hated that. I wished I hadn't gotten myself into this situation, but I couldn't go back and change it, so I just had to deal with it.

I had no idea if Veronica and Cynthia would be back from

visiting Aggie yet, but I figured I'd be safe to head to the church office for a little while without them if they were still out and about.

Pastor Coker was seated in my desk chair when I entered, and our youth pastor, Greg, was at his desk across from mine.

"What are you two doing here?"

Pastor Coker replied, "Veronica stopped by the house a little bit ago and asked me to come over here in case you dropped by before she and Cynthia got back."

Greg explained, "I was heading into The Check when I noticed the light on in here and came over to investigate, since the place is usually empty on Fridays. We've just been talking about the murder and who might've done it."

My eyebrows rose. "Yeah? And who might that be?"

Pastor Coker started to rise from my chair so I could sit, but I waved him back down and took one of the guest chairs instead.

Greg raised his hand. "I think it's the son. I heard he and his dad were on the outs."

"I vote for the daughter," Pastor Coker said. "She and her husband are separated, and he recently lost his job. I think they need money, and she thought her inheritance would answer all her problems."

I cocked my head to the side. "Yeah, but she loved her dad."

"People do crazy things," Greg stated. "And everybody's saying that nobody knew John changed his will."

My body jolted when that comment triggered thoughts of Donnie Masters. "Oh, no! I forgot to tell Mitchell what we found out about Donnie." I hoped Marty would remember to tell him, but if I didn't think about it, maybe he didn't, either.

"What did you find out about Donnie?" Pastor Coker asked.

"I'll tell you in a minute. I need to call the bank and try to catch Mitchell."

I snatched up my desk phone and dialed the bank's phone number.

"Cherry County Bank, how may I help you?" my mom's voice greeted me.

"Hey, Mom, is Mitchell still there?" He should be, since he'd only been there a handful of minutes.

"Well, hello, to you, too."

"Hi. Hello. How are you? Now, please answer my question."

"Mitchell, Nancy, and Marty are in Jeff's office."

"Good. When they come out, will you tell Marty I called to remind him to tell Mitchell about Donnie?"

She hummed in response. "I'll tell him that if you tell *me* about Donnie."

I took a deep breath. "Mother."

"Yes, dear?"

"Do you want Marty to go to jail?"

Mom sighed. "No, but I don't see why you can't tell me what you know."

"I can tell you, and I will in just a second, but this isn't a negotiation. Mitchell needs to know what we found out."

"All right, keep your pants on. You know I'll tell him. Now, tell me."

Before I could start, I realized Marty didn't know everything, either. "No, I need to come down there and talk to both of the guys. Marty doesn't know everything, because I learned a few new things after I left him at home this morning."

Pastor Coker's mouth dropped open at that statement. I held up a finger to him, letting him know I'd explain in a minute.

"Just tell me, and I can tell them," Mom said.

"No." I shake my head. "I'm coming down there."

"Beckett—"

"I'm coming, Mother. See you in a minute. Don't let the guys leave before I get there."

I hung up the phone and announced to the room, "Both Kyle and Marty spent the night at my house to ensure my safety with a killer on the loose. Not," I pointed my finger at each of them, "that it's any of your business who spends the night at my house."

Greg held both hands up in surrender. "I said nothing."

"I know. I'm just saying."

I grabbed my purse and coat from the back of my chair and marched out of the office.

When I entered the bank a minute later, I made a beeline for Jeff's office. The door was shut, and the blinds were closed on the floor-to-ceiling window, making me assume the three men and Nancy were still in there.

"Beckett!" my mom called out. "Don't go in there. Jeff said not to disturb them."

I snorted. "I'd like to see any of them try to throw me out of there."

A chuckle filtered out of the office next to Jeff's. I glanced in to see the bank's president, Perry Adamson, eating a donut at his desk.

I paused for just a moment at his door. "Hey, Perry. You doing all right?" He was shot in this very bank last fall, and he'd only been back to work for a few weeks. He was easing back in, only spending a few hours a day at the office.

"Right as rain, Becky." He used his donut to motion toward Jeff's office. "Go on in. They won't mind."

I tapped the door frame and gave him a sunny smile. "Thanks."

I knocked on Jeff's office door and opened it before waiting for a response. Nancy didn't react to my presence, but all three men looked at me with different expressions on their faces. Jeff grinned and shook his head. Marty's eyebrows drew together in a look of concern. Mitchell narrowed his eyes at me. I was not surprised by any of this.

"Can we help you, Ms. Monahan?" Jeff asked, grin still firmly in place.

"As a matter of fact, you can." I shut the door behind me, and Jeff stood and motioned for me to take his seat. I dropped down onto the cushy leather chair and swiveled back and forth a couple times.

"Well ... ?" Mitchell prompted.

"I forgot to tell you what we found out about Donnie this morning." I looked at Marty. "Did you tell him? I also learned something else that you don't know yet."

Marty shook his head. "No, I hadn't gotten around to it."

Mitchell moved his hand in a rolling motion. "Go ahead, Beckett."

I explained about the gambling theory and Donnie's VFW connection.

"We had put two and two together on the VFW thing," Mitchell said, "but we didn't know about the gambling. Thanks. If that's all, you can go."

Leaving was the last thing I intended to do now that I was here. "Did you find out if anyone tried to withdraw money from the store's account yesterday or today?"

"Not yet," Jeff said. "I'll talk to your mom and call Aggie, since they were the only tellers here yesterday, but I can't imagine either of them would ever let anyone but you," he nodded toward Marty, "or John withdraw money from the account without talking to me or Perry about it. You two are the only people with authorized access to the funds." He shrugged. "And I'm guessing you didn't take any money out, Marty, or you wouldn't be here right now asking this question."

"Absolutely not," Marty replied with a frown. "I've never taken money out of the store's account that wasn't for a bill or my paycheck. Feel free to look through the books if you need proof."

"I wish I could take your word for it," Mitchell said, "but I need to do my due diligence and take a look. I also need to talk to Minda and the other tellers directly to make sure nobody else has withdrawn money from the account or even inquired about it." He waved his finger between Nancy, Marty, and me. "You three can go. Thanks for your help this morning. I need to ask Jeff a few more questions before I talk to the ladies and then head back to the station."

I gave Jeff a side hug before following Marty and Nancy out of the office. Mitchell made eye contact with me but didn't say anything else as he closed the door behind me.

Mom waved us over to her window, so we crossed the lobby to her.

She said in a low voice, "If you can stay for a few minutes, I'll take my break so we can chat in the break room. I want to know what you know, and I need to tell you what happened just a few minutes ago."

"Mitchell needs to talk to you when he leaves Jeff's office," I said.

"And I need to talk to him." She looked over the half wall to the young woman in the next teller booth. "Kaley, you good on your own out here for a few minutes? It's usually pretty slow at this time of the morning."

"Sure, Mrs. Monahan. Go on." Kaley smiled at all of us. She'd only been working at the bank for a month or so, but she seemed sweet and was a good worker, according to my mom.

"If Detective Crowe comes out in the meantime, send him to the break room," Mom ordered her as she locked up her money drawer. "I have some news for him."

"Will do."

After we headed to the break room and settled around the small table, I gave everyone the lowdown on everything I'd learned since I last talked to each of them. When I was almost finished, Mitchell entered the room.

Mom patted the table in front of the empty chair. "Have a seat. I have something to tell you."

"And I have something to ask you." He dropped down into the chair with a sigh. He looked like he hadn't slept much, which wasn't surprising. I appreciated how hard he was working to find the real killer.

"Paul Kemper came through the drive-thru while you four were in Jeff's office," Mom said.

"He what?" Mitchell exclaimed. "Why didn't you tell me?"

"I'm telling you now," my mother said in an exasperated voice. "And if you recall, you told me not to bother you."

He snorts. "That didn't stop your daughter."

"Hey!" I glared at him.

"Minda, why don't you tell us what happened," Marty said calmly to my mom. Leave it to the prime suspect to be the voice of reason.

Chapter Thirteen

"Like I said," Mom explained, "Paul came through the drive-thru while you were in your meeting. He gave me a slip of paper with an account number on it and said he needed five thousand dollars withdrawn from that account. I was suspicious to say the least, so I asked whose account that was. He got mad and told me to just give him the money because it rightfully belonged to him. Of course I refused, and I informed him a police officer was in the bank. That put the fear of God in him, and he peeled out." She sighed. "Now I realize I should've tried to keep him there and somehow gotten word to you in Jeff's office, but I wasn't thinking straight."

"No, you did the right thing," Mitchell said. "He could've had a weapon. It's best to leave any further interactions with him to the police." He gave me a stern look.

"What are you looking at me for?" I asked innocently.

"Anyway," Nancy interjected, "Minda, I'm sure you looked up whose account that was after he left. Was it John's or the store's or someone else's?"

"It was the store's checking account," Mom said. "John still has a personal account here, even though he moved, but there's only a few hundred in it."

"Well," Marty said, "Paul wouldn't have gotten five grand out of the store's account, because there's not that much in there now. But," he swept his gaze around to each of us, "the latest statement—the one in that file," he pointed to the bag at Mitchell's feet, "showed around fifty-one hundred. Paychecks went out since the statement, and I paid the monthly bill to a few suppliers, so the current balance is around three thousand."

"That doesn't seem like a coincidence to me," I stated.

"No, it doesn't," Mitchell said, "but it's also not proof of anything. It's a round amount that could've been a lucky guess. And if we don't find any fingerprints on the file or desk, we still won't be able to prove he was in the office and looked at the bank statement."

I groaned and dropped my head into my hands. "We've got to find credible evidence against somebody other than Marty!"

"How much longer do you think we have before you'll have to arrest Marty?" Nancy asked Mitchell.

Tears filled my eyes at her question and the resigned look on Marty's face. I wanted to comfort him, but I couldn't do so in front of Mitchell.

"I'm going to hold off as long as I can, but probably not more than another day if we can't find evidence pointing to someone else. I'm sorry." To Mitchell's credit, he looked troubled by the thought.

"What will you do about the store?" I asked Marty. "What can we do to help keep the doors open if you can't?"

Marty shook his head. "I don't know. Todd's the only full-time employee, but he's only nineteen and isn't ready to run the place. And while I trust my part-timers, they don't have the potential to run things. I'm also now the only person who can sign checks for payroll and bills. I think it'll just have to stay closed."

"You'll have to add someone else to the bank account," Mom said. "Bills will keep coming even if the store is closed, and you'll need to pay your workers for their hours since their last paychecks. Surely you can find someone else you trust to keep the store running. Your dad, maybe?"

"My dad is a good man, but he doesn't have a head for business. I'm sure he'd agree to help out in any way he can, but I don't want to put that kind of pressure on him if I don't need to."

"What about Beckett?" Mitchell suggested.

We all gaped at him.

"What?" He held his hands out palm up and then addressed Marty. "We all know she's completely trustworthy. She's not going to steal your money or run your store into the ground, and she went to business school." He looked at me. "You're more than capable of running a business, even if you can't be there all the time because of your job."

As the shock wore off, I realized his idea wasn't terrible. "Yeah, I like this idea."

I nodded in agreement with myself, and Marty was nodding along with me.

I said, "I can open up and close every day, and I can keep an eye on things from across the street while I'm at work and run over during lunch and my other breaks." I allowed myself to reach over and cover Marty's hand with my own. "That way your employees can keep working and getting paid, and the people of Cherry Hill can keep getting their hardware supplies here in town and support you in the process. Nobody thinks you did this, Marty. *No one.* There's no reason for you to lose your business because of this mess."

"It's still strange that it's now my business." He huffed out a short laugh. "Not that I didn't already run it as if it were my own, but it's different now that I know it's all on me and there's nobody else to fall back on if things go wrong. And things have sure enough gone wrong from the start."

Mitchell pushed up from the table. "I'm going to leave you all here to see what you can work out with the store if worst comes to worst. I need to get back to the station and see if anyone has come up with any more leads."

Marty and I left the bank an hour later with a plan for me to run the business starting Monday if it came down to that. We also both signed paperwork adding my name to the store's bank account. It meant a lot to me that he trusted me enough to do that. It also meant a lot that the whole idea had come from Mitchell, considering the dynamics between the three of us.

More than anything else, though, it felt *right* that I was doing this for Marty. Potentially running his business could've felt scary or impossible or even like I was being trapped into something I didn't want—when it came to both my job and my relationship with Marty. But I was excited—not excited about the reason for it but for the opportunity to put my associate's degree to good use and stretch myself to do something I might never have done if left to my own devices.

I was relatively happy in my job at First Community Church. It was comfortable, and I was good at it. But I wasn't in charge of anything, really, and I couldn't make many decisions. I had a lot of ideas for programs and events that never went anywhere because the deacons didn't think they were worth pursuing.

"Beckett," Marty said as he walked me back down the street to the church office, "can we talk? I mean, about us? It's okay if you're not ready, but we might not have much time." He stopped in front of the church door and stuck his hands in his jacket pockets. "I'm pretty sure I won't end up being in jail long, because I trust both you and Mitchell to find the real killer. But I'd like to know where things stand between us before I'm arrested. I want to know what I'll be coming home to when I get out."

Tears pricked behind my eyes at his words and the uncertainty in his eyes. "Yeah, you deserve to know how I feel. I need to run in here and update the guys and let them know I'm going home. Let's meet at my house in twenty minutes?"

He nodded. "Yeah, that sounds good." He looked at his watch. "It's almost lunch time. Want me to pick something up?"

It was kind of him to ask, but I didn't want to subject him to having to talk to anyone while picking up food for us.

"I've got stuff for sandwiches at home. If that's fine with you, that's fine with me."

"Yeah. I'm gonna stop by and see my dad before I head to your house."

I placed a hand on his arm. "Tell him I said hi. I'll see you soon."

Marty opened the door for me, and I gave him a smile and a reassuring pat on his chest as I passed by.

As soon as I re-entered the church office, Greg said, "Edna Thorn came by while you were gone. She said she's been trying to track you down all day but you've always been a step ahead of her. She wants you to stop by and see her because she has something pressing to tell you that could help solve the murder."

"Has she told the police?"

Pastor Coker nodded. "Yes, and she thinks they're taking her information seriously enough, but she also wanted you to know, since she wasn't sure they'd tell you about it."

"Edna," I said as I entered the fifty-something newspaper editor's cluttered office, "what do I need to know?"

She swept her hand toward the lone guest chair, which hosted a tower of magazines and newspapers. "Just set those anywhere and have a seat."

I transferred the periodicals to the floor and perched on the edge of the cracked orange vinyl seat.

"All day yesterday," she said, "I had a niggling feeling I knew something that would help solve this murder. As I told you, I don't believe Marty James has it in him to kill a person ... ," she cocked her head to the side and perused me for a second, "unless he felt it was the only option in order to protect someone he loves." She shook her head. "But I digress. This morning it came to me. A few months ago I was in Springfield and met an old college friend for dinner. Across the room, I saw a woman who I'm ninety-nine percent certain was Paul's wife, though I never got close enough to know with absolute certainty. She was with a man, and she was definitely *with* him, if you know what I mean, but he most definitely was not Paul."

"Okay." I tapped my lips with my pointer finger. "That doesn't look good for Paul's marriage, but how does that help us with the murder investigation?"

"It could be related to motive and perhaps opportunity. Maybe he's gearing up for a divorce and needs cash. Or maybe his wife wasn't home the night of the murder because she was with the mystery man, but she doesn't want to admit that to the police, so she guessed at whether Paul was home all night. Or," she held up a finger, "she's the one who killed John, because she wanted Paul to get the inheritance before she divorced him, so she could try to get part of it. The possibilities are endless."

"All right. I'll think on that. Thanks for letting me know."

I started to stand but Edna waved me back down.

"Did you know John and Suzanne LaHaye were seeing each other?" she asked. "I heard that late last night."

"Yes, I heard that this morning and had completely forgotten! I need to go talk to Suzanne. I can't believe she hasn't contacted me." I hit my temple with my palm. "Dang it! I didn't tell Mitchell about that."

"No need. I mentioned it when I talked to Frank earlier. Now, have you learned anything else since we last spoke?"

I told her what we found at the store earlier and that Paul had tried to withdraw money at the bank. Then I hesitated before asking, "Do you think Donnie Masters could've had anything to do with it?"

Edna's eyebrows rose. "You think Donnie might've killed John? Why?"

"No concrete reason yet, but it could've been financial. It

seems he might have a gambling issue, and Kathleen told me her dad left twenty-five grand to the VFW."

Edna let out a low whistle. "That's a lot of money. And Donnie's the VFW treasurer."

"Exactly."

"All right, I'll talk to some of the other men in the VFW that I trust and see if there's been anything strange going on with their finances. I'll let you know if I learn anything useful."

I nodded and tilted my head toward Edna. "Anything else you need to tell me?"

She shooed me away with her hand. "No, go find who did this. Talk to Suzanne and see what she might know. I've tried calling her multiple times, but I haven't gotten an answer."

As I hurried back to my car, I was torn about what to do next. I needed to meet Marty at my house in five minutes, but I also needed to talk to Suzanne about John. However, I didn't want to keep Marty waiting, so I decided I'd go ahead and talk to him, and then maybe we could go talk to Suzanne together.

Marty's truck was parked in my driveway when I got home, and he climbed out of it when I pulled in. I rolled my window down as I waited for the garage door to go up.

"You didn't have to wait out here," I said. "I gave you a key."

"You gave me a key so I could lock up this morning, not so I could come and go as I please." He shrugged. "I didn't want to take advantage."

I nodded. "I appreciate that." Then I pulled into the garage, and we headed into the house together. He watched as the garage door closed, likely making sure nobody snuck in while we weren't paying attention, which I also appreciated.

"Let's eat first, and then we'll talk," I said.

I bustled around the kitchen getting everything out for the sandwiches along with some chips and drinks, and we made small talk while we fixed our sandwiches and began eating. Marty didn't make eye contact with me the entire time, so as soon as he took the last bite of his sandwich, I decided it was time to put him out of his misery.

"When I decided to take this break," I explained, "Aunt Star said something that really stuck with me. She encouraged me to not simply choose between you and Mitchell but to decide what I wanted for my future and then see if I could envision one of you in that future with me. So it hasn't just been about picking one of you over the other. It's been about me deciding what's best for me, even if that meant not being with either of you. Does that make sense?"

Marty nodded. "It does. It was great advice. I wouldn't want you to decide to be with me only because you thought I was a better option than Mitchell. I want you to choose me because I'm *me* and you can't see your future with anyone else."

"I'll be honest," I said, "I wasn't sure what I was going to do as recently as yesterday. While I needed some time away from both of you to think, I've realized I couldn't make this decision without spending time with both of you again."

He appeared to be holding his breath, so I didn't make him wait any longer.

"I've also realized that the person I see my future with is *you.*"

Marty let out his breath and then closed his eyes as a smile spread across his face. When he opened his eyes, his expression was a strange mixture of relief and apprehension. I reached my hand across the table, and he grasped it in his.

"I don't think I need to tell you I see my future with you, too," he said, "but right now that future is so uncertain." His voice trembled a little as he asked, "Are you sure you want to choose me?"

I let go of his hand so I could round the table to him. He turned sideways in his chair, and I stepped between his legs and cupped his cheeks in my hands.

"I'm positive. Even if you find yourself living temporarily at the Cherry County Jail, I choose you."

His hands landed on my hips. "And I choose you. I don't expect you to say this back to me yet, but since I don't know when I could be taken from you, I need to tell you that I love you, Beckett Monahan. And this time I'm not saying it under the influence of high-powered painkillers."

I chuckled as my thumbs stroked his cheeks. "I love you, too, Marty James. I love your kind heart and your loyalty. I love your steadiness and your thoughtfulness. And I'd also love for you to kiss me right now."

In response, he pulled me down onto his lap and cradled the back of my head in his hand. "I've been waiting a long time to do this." And then he kissed me.

Chapter Fourteen

M arty kissed me like he ... well, like he might be going off to prison and didn't know when he might see me again. I'd never been kissed so thoroughly in my life. After a few minutes, he stood and led me into the living room so we could continue making out on the couch like a couple of teenagers.

While my body was telling me to spend the rest of the day curled up on the couch with him, my brain knew we needed to get back to our investigation so he wouldn't be going off to prison. More specifically, we needed to go talk to Suzanne.

Reluctantly, I drew my mouth away from his after what could've been five minutes or fifty. I had no idea which was more accurate.

"Wow. That was ... wow."

Marty grinned and trailed a finger along my jawline. "My thoughts exactly."

"As much as I hate to put a stop to this, it's more important that we clear your name. Want to come with me to see Suzanne? Word on the street is she and John were dating."

His eyebrows shot up. "What? Are you serious?"

"I heard it from both Callie and Edna. John never said anything to you?"

Marty shook his head slowly. "No, but I guess it makes sense ... kinda ... maybe."

I laughed. "You don't sound very sure."

"I'm not, actually, but that doesn't mean it's not true. We'd better go see what Suzanne might have to say. I'm surprised she didn't try to talk to you already."

"Me, too. I'm planning to ask her why she didn't."

He stood and pulled me up beside him before wrapping his arms back around me. "I expect nothing less." He pressed a hard kiss to my lips. "Let's go, then, before I pull you back down onto that couch with me."

While I bundled myself back up in preparation for going out into the cold, Marty seemed like he wanted to say something but was hesitating for some reason.

"What?" I asked. "I can tell you have something to say."

"I was wondering if we shouldn't tell anyone about us yet." He pointed his finger back and forth between us. "I mean, I want to shout it to the heavens, but do you want to talk to Mitchell before we tell anyone else? That only seems fair."

I went up onto my tiptoes to give him a quick kiss. "See? This is one of the many reasons I want to be with you. Instead of wanting to rub it in, you care about his feelings."

He shrugged. "I'm just thinking about how I would feel if the tables were turned. And while I know I should maybe be worried that this will make him not work so hard to find other evidence that would take the spotlight off me, I don't think that's going to happen. He's a good man and a good detective. I can't see him letting his feelings get in the way of justice. And I don't want you to wait to tell him until this case is resolved. He deserves to know, even if there's a slight chance that could backfire on me."

I patted him on the chest. "The way you two have chosen to respect instead of resent each other makes my heart happy."

He smiled. "Ready to go?"

"Wait. Maybe we should call Suzanne instead of just stopping by unannounced."

He shook his head as he opened the door into the garage and ushered me out. "Knowing Suzanne, she's not answering her phone right now. She's always happy to talk about other people's lives, but something tells me she doesn't want to talk about this."

My chest squeezed. "She's probably grieving, too."

Marty's face dropped at this comment. "I feel bad I haven't been able to do that. John was one of my closest friends."

I took both of his hands in mine as we stood behind my car in the open garage. "I know, and that's yet another reason I want to get this case solved as quickly as possible."

The sound of a car approaching caused us both to look out to the driveway, where Mitchell's truck was pulling in. Marty pulled his hands out of mine and slipped them into his pockets.

"Busted," I muttered. While I knew the conversation with Mitchell about our relationship was imminent, I wasn't prepared to have it quite yet.

"Are you here for me?" Marty asked when Mitchell stepped out of his pickup.

"No." Mitchell looked back and forth between the two of us and cleared his throat. "I came by because I saw your vehicles in the drive and wanted to know if either of you have seen or heard from Suzanne in the last two days."

My eyebrows jumped. "You don't know where she is? We were just headed over to her house to talk to her."

Mitchell leaned back against the grill of his truck and crossed his arms over his chest. "Why did you want to talk to her?"

"Because apparently she was dating John, which I know you know." I placed a fist on my hip. "But you didn't answer my question."

"No, we don't know where she is. Frank tried calling her this morning with no luck, so I decided to stop by her house, but nobody answered the door."

"Maybe she just doesn't want to talk to anyone about it?" I guessed.

"She could be out of town," Marty said. "Have you checked

with Jacqui?" Surely Suzanne's daughter would know if her mother had left town.

"Not yet. That's where I was headed when I decided to check in with you two." Mitchell's gaze bounced between me and Marty again.

Before Mitchell could say anything else, Marty jumped in, "If you don't need anything else from me, I'm going to head to my parents' house for a while."

He gave me a look that said, "Now's the time to talk to him," and I nodded.

"Fine by me," Mitchell replied.

He and I were silent as Marty said goodbye and left.

"Can we talk for a minute?" I asked him. "Inside? I know you're trying to track down Suzanne, but this will only take a few minutes."

Mitchell nodded once and then headed toward the door from the garage into the house. He hit the button for the overhead garage door once I was clear of it.

"Can't be too careful," he said. My heart clenched at how he was thinking of my safety even when he knew what I was about to tell him.

"Let's talk in the kitchen," I said.

Although it was strange to be having this conversation in the same place I had the one with Marty thirty minutes ago, I didn't feel it was appropriate to have it on the couch where I'd just been kissing the face off my new boyfriend.

We took our coats off before taking our seats across from each other, and Mitchell gave me a sad smile.

"I think you know what I'm about to say."

He nodded. "Yeah, but I'm gonna let you say it anyway."

I took a deep breath. "I care about you a lot. We've had some great times together, and I think you're a wonderful man."

"But ... ," he said with a sigh.

"But I just don't see a future for us. I want a life of stability close to my family. I want to live here in Cherry Hill surrounded by people I know and love. And I realized after the conversation this morning that I want to try running a business, whether that's the hardware store or something else. I can't do that if I'm potentially moving every few years. You want to advance in your career, which is understandable, and I'd want to support that if I were with you. But that equals instability in many ways, and that's not what I want for my life."

He nodded. "I understand. I do. I'm not happy about it, because I love you and I wanted to see if we could go the distance. But I get it. And I'm honestly not surprised, after seeing you and Marty together today. The way you look at him ...," he briefly closed his eyes, "you've never looked at me that way."

Tears filled my eyes. "I'm sorry, Mitchell."

"Me, too."

The look he gave me was so tender the tears spilled down onto my cheeks.

"Don't cry, Beckett." He leaned his chair back so he could grab the tissue box off the counter behind him. "I don't want you to be sad. I want you to have everything you've ever wanted. And if that includes Marty, then that's what I want for you, as much as it may hurt."

His words made me cry even harder. "You'll find someone who's perfect for you," I said between sniffles. "Maybe things can still work out between you and Chris. Is she doing okay after the accident?" Mitchell's lifelong best friend was in a terrible accident right before Christmas.

The corners of his mouth curved up and a spark lit in his eyes. "Yeah, she's recovering faster than expected and got her leg cast removed last week. She was able to go back to teaching part-time on Monday."

"Good. I'm glad she's on the mend. After you've had some time to process this, I want you to reconsider whether she might be the one for you, all right? I want you to be happy, too. And judging from the smile on your face, I think she just might be the one to make you truly happy."

Chapter Fifteen

"Now," I clapped my hands together, "I know you probably don't want to dwell on this, so let's get on with this case." I pointed at the phone on the wall. "Even though it will mean being in my presence a little longer, why don't you try calling Jacqui from here, instead of going to her house? She's probably at work right now. I heard she got a job at the candle factory in Jefferson City. Doubt it'll last long, considering her track record."

I stood and grabbed the phone book to look up Jacqui's number while Mitchell slowly got to his feet. I felt for him, I truly did, but sitting around and moping wasn't going to solve anything.

When I found the number, I dialed it and gave the handset to Mitchell. As predicted, nobody answered. He left a message on her answering machine asking her to call the police station when she got home.

"Let's try Veronica now," I suggested. "She was as surprised as anyone when we heard about John and Suzanne this morning. Maybe she tried going over to Suzanne's after she and Cynthia left The Check. If nothing else, she might know where Suzanne keeps her spare key so we can get in the house and make sure Suzanne's not in there and is sick or hurt."

Mitchell shook his head. "I can't really be part of that."

"That's fine. Veronica and I can be the ones to go in the house if it comes to it, but at least wait here while I call and see if Veronica knows where Suzanne is."

He leaned against the counter while I dialed the parsonage. Veronica answered on the second ring.

"Hey, it's me. How's Adam doing? Is Aggie managing okay?"

"Yes, Adam's going to be fine. He's a little croupy but nothing to be concerned about. Aggie just has new mom jitters. Any little thing can be worrisome with your first baby."

"Oh good, I'm glad he's not too sick. Anyway, I'm calling to ask if you've seen or talked to Suzanne today." I cocked my head. "Or yesterday, for that matter."

"No, I haven't. I tried calling a few times but she didn't answer. I intend to go over this afternoon and ask why she didn't tell me about her and John. Do you want to go with me? Cynthia and I are eating lunch now, but we can pick you up in fifteen or twenty minutes."

I sneaked a peek at Mitchell, who was fidgeting impatiently. "Yes, I'd like to talk to her, but nobody seems to know where she is, including the police, so I don't want to wait that long."

"Oh! That's not good."

"Do you know if she was planning to go out of town?"

"No, but apparently she doesn't tell me everything. I'm worried, though. And if she isn't home, we need to find out how to get word to her about John. You tried Jacqui?"

"Yes, I'm guessing she's at work." I tapped my fingers on the countertop.

"Okay, we can be at your house in five minutes."

"Sounds good. Do you know where Suzanne keeps her spare key?"

"I do. See you soon."

Mitchell pushed off the counter as I hung up.

"You want to go over there with us?" I asked. "Veronica knows where the key is."

"I'm heading back to the station. Call if Suzanne's home so we can talk to her." He bobbed his head back and forth. "Also call if she's not home, because we need to find her whether she knows anything about this or not." He bit the inside of his cheek, and his eyes filled with concern. "It's not like her to not be in the middle of anything big happening in town."

My eyes grew wide as I followed him to the front door. "You don't think she's ..."

He shrugged as he opened the door. "I don't want to think the worst, but we have to consider it. Call me from Suzanne's house no matter what you find." He stopped. "On second thought, I *should* probably be there if nobody answers the door and you need to go in."

I swallowed thickly as I considered what we might discover at Suzanne's house. "I'd appreciate that, especially since my cousin will be with us."

Mitchell's eyebrows raised. "Your cousin?"

"Yeah, my seventeen-year-old cousin is here visiting from Arkansas. She stayed with my parents last night, but she's hanging out with Veronica today while my parents are at work."

"You sure you want her involved in this?"

I shrugged. "Not really, but she's already involved. And if you're with us at Suzanne's, I'm not worried about her safety. But if we find ..." I trailed that thought off.

"Yeah, we need to make sure she doesn't see anything that might scar her for life."

"Exactly," I said. "While we wait, do you need to use the phone to check in with the station about anything?"

Mitchell shook his head. "No, I'll do it from the radio in my car." He paused and then closed the door without going outside. "Actually, I'll use the phone. That way nobody else can potentially listen in. I need to update the team about Suzanne, but I don't want the whole town hearing about it."

He disappeared back into the kitchen to call the station while I watched for Veronica's car out the picture window. I kept my ears open, though, to see if I'd learn anything I didn't already know.

His conversation was short and uninformative, and he soon joined me at the window. It was strange to be that close to him but not be touching him. I knew I'd made the right choice, but I was going to miss the man standing beside me. I really hoped he could make things work with Chris.

"Was my suggestion that you run the hardware store the thing that tipped you over the edge?" he asked quietly.

I shook my head. "No. That helped solidify my decision, but I'd already decided I was going to stay in Cherry Hill long-term and give things a try with Marty. I just didn't know when I'd tell the two of you. But with Marty potentially going to jail, that forced the timeline. It might seem weird to some people that I'd declare my intention to date a man suspected of murder, but we both know he didn't do it."

"I'm doing everything I can to clear his name. You know that, right?"

I reached over and squeezed his arm. "I know. You're a good man and a good detective. You'll figure it out."

He huffed out a laugh. "Or you will."

Veronica's car pulled up to the curb outside my house, and we headed out. Mitchell double checked that the door was locked before following me down the sidewalk. Veronica rolled her window down as we approached, and she shot me a questioning look.

I pointed my thumb over my shoulder at Mitchell. "He's going to follow us over there. If we need to use the key to go inside, he'll be there in case anything's not right."

Her shoulders slumped. "I hope everything's all right, but I'm afraid that's not the case."

"We'll find out soon enough," Mitchell said as he headed to his truck.

I got into Veronica's car, and as soon as my door closed, she asked, "Have you made your decision?"

"What decision?" Cynthia piped up from the backseat, before shoving her face between the front seats.

I shot Veronica a look, and she mouthed, "Sorry," to me.

"My decision about whether to keep investigating," I said.

"Why would you stop?" my cousin demanded. "You need to find who did this so Marty doesn't get framed!"

I smiled at her outrage. "Yes, I do. So I'm not going to stop."

"Good."

We stopped at the curb at Suzanne's house, and Mitchell pulled up behind us. When nobody answered either the front or back door, and we couldn't see anybody through any of the windows, Veronica made the rest of us turn our backs while she procured the spare backdoor key from its hiding place.

She turned the key in the lock and took a deep breath. "Detective Crowe, would you like to go in first?"

He nodded. "I think that would be for the best. We'll go in, and you and Beckett can call out for her, but I'll be the first to go through any doorway, all right? Cynthia, I need you to stay in the kitchen. Don't touch anything if you can help it."

We followed Mitchell in, he locked the door behind us, and Veronica called out Suzanne's name, but we didn't hear a response. He led us through the ground floor and then upstairs to the bedrooms, which were all empty. I felt a huge sense of relief that we didn't find Suzanne hurt or worse, but I also couldn't imagine where she might be. Surely she was somewhere she hadn't yet heard about John, or she'd have come home or at least called Veronica.

"I'm going to go back down and check the basement and garage," Mitchell said as we stood in the middle of Suzanne's bedroom. "And I'm not officially asking you to do this, but it could be helpful if someone maybe did a little snooping to see if it looks like she recently packed a bag or two for a trip. That could help us determine whether she's out of town and whether she intended to be."

"You check the bathroom," I told Veronica, "and I'll check the closet. Do you have any idea where she keeps her suitcase?"

"I do not." She stepped into the attached bathroom, and within seconds she was back out. "The toothbrush holder is empty. I'd say that'a a pretty good sign she's out of town. I just don't know why she didn't tell me."

Through the open closet door, I could see an empty suitcase-sized spot on the shelf above the hanging clothes. "Looks like a suitcase is gone, too. I don't think we need to snoop any further."

"So what does this mean?" I asked Mitchell a minute later when we reconvened in the kitchen and we told him what we found—or didn't find.

"It means she likely left town of her own free will, which is good. But it also means we can't verify her whereabouts at the time of the murder." He held his hands up in defense, knowing we'd have something to say about that. "I don't believe she killed John, but the partner is always a suspect. I don't know how serious their relationship was, but we have to consider her."

I plopped down into a chair at the kitchen table. "And we still don't have any evidence against anyone other than Marty."

I dropped my head onto my hands on the tabletop, and Veronica rubbed my back.

"On that note," Mitchell said, and I raised my head to look at him, "I need to get back to the station and see if there are updates from anyone else that could help, and hopefully we've received the full coroner's report by now. I'll leave you three to whatever else you think you might want to do here. Just make sure to lock up when you leave. And if you forget to put the key back, I wouldn't complain."

"Wait a minute," I said. "Yesterday, did the coroner have any idea of what time John was killed?"

"He estimated no more than two hours before he arrived,

which was around 7:30." Then he said goodbye and exited through the back door.

"It just doesn't make any sense." I pounded a fist on the table. "Why would John and someone else have been in the store at 5:30 in the morning?"

"I have no idea." Veronica stood. "But we're going to search this house high and low for any sign of where Suzanne might've gone."

She crossed the kitchen to where the phone hung on the wall. "Maybe we can find a note somewhere that will help determine where she went and for how long." She started sorting through a pile of papers on the counter under the phone.

"There's a calendar over there on the wall," Cynthia said. "That could be helpful."

She pointed, and Veronica moved over to it. "Not sure why this wasn't the first thing we looked for."

She ran her fingers along the dates. "No mention of going anywhere this week, but on last Thursday and Friday, it says 'J.K.'"

"John Kemper," I stated unnecessarily.

"She called me last Thursday night!" Veronica crossed her arms over her chest as she turned to me. "She was with John and didn't say a word!"

I felt for my friend, but this wasn't the time for her to get worked up about Suzanne's secret keeping. "And you can address that with her when you see her again. But for now, we need to figure out where she is."

"You're right." Veronica checked her watch. "It'll probably be a few more hours before Jacqui gets off work."

"Where else would Suzanne go, and why?" I asked. "She obviously didn't go visit John, because he was here. Does she have family anywhere else? Or friends she visits?"

Veronica dropped down into the chair across from me. "She doesn't have siblings, and her parents are long gone. She's not originally from Cherry Hill, but she's lived here more than thirty years now—since her early twenties. There's an elderly aunt she sometimes visits, but I don't know her name or how to contact her."

"She should have an address book somewhere," Cynthia said. "That might help."

"It would if we knew who to look for," I said.

My eyes bounced around the room again, searching for anything that might give us a clue. I noticed the phone in the kitchen didn't have an answering machine attached, but I knew Suzanne had one, because I'd left messages on it.

I stood. "Where's her answering machine?"

Veronica stood up straight. "In the living room. You want to listen to her messages? Is that legal?"

"I can't imagine there's an actual law against it, but at this point I don't really care."

I made my way into the living room and spied the phone and answering machine on an end table next to the couch. The red light was blinking on the machine. I stood there staring at it for a moment before Veronica moved around me with a pen and notepad in her hand.

"Might as well get it over with." She hit the "play" button, and John Kemper's voice filled the room.

Chapter Sixteen

"Suzanne, honey," John's voice said through the answering machine as Veronica and I stared at each other with open mouths, "I'm coming to Cherry Hill tonight and plan to stay a couple nights. Paul wants to meet me there for reasons he didn't explain, but you know I'm hoping to patch things up with him, so I said I'd come, though I don't know why we can't do this here in Springfield. Anyway, the hotel doesn't have any available rooms, so I hope it's okay for me to stay in your guest room. If not, we'll figure something else out when I get there. It'll be late by the time I arrive. I love you, pumpkin, and I'll see you soon."

When the machine clicked off, I said, "We've gotta get Mitchell back over here." I picked up the phone and dialed the station, and Barbara answered on the second ring. "Barbara, this is Beckett. Is Mitchell back there yet? I have something extremely important to tell him."

Oddly, she didn't give me any grief like she usually did. "I can see him pulling into the lot now. I'll put you on hold."

"Wait! Can you just tell him to get back over to Suzanne's right now? We found some evidence."

"Is Suzanne there? Did you track her down?" Barbara actually sounded worried, which was uncommon.

"No, but I need you tell Mitchell to come back immediately, please."

"Will do, Becky. I'll catch him before he even comes in the door. Bye." She hung up before I could reply.

"Don't touch anything else before Mitchell gets here," Veronica ordered. "We don't know what other evidence might be hidden in plain sight."

"Good idea, but I'm still gonna snoop without touching anything. Did you see any sign that John might've stayed here overnight, even if Suzanne wasn't here?"

Veronica pursed her lips. "I noticed the bedspread on the bed in the front guest room was a little rumpled. Suzanne usually keeps things so neat, that stood out to me."

I headed for the stairs. "Let's see if we can find anything of John's in there or in the hall bathroom. If he stayed here, I can't imagine he took everything with him when he left to go to the store before the crack of dawn. He would've assumed he'd be coming back, even if Suzanne wasn't here, since The Osh was fully booked." The Oak Street Hotel, locally known as The Osh, was our town's only hotel.

The others followed me upstairs and Veronica pointed Cynthia and me toward the guest room in question, while she moved farther down to the bathroom. The bed was made, but not with the precision Suzanne is known for in every aspect of her life, and the sliding closet door wasn't closed all the way. Cynthia spotted it too, and she used her elbow to open it further, revealing an open duffel bag on the floor. She crouched down next to it, taking care not to touch anything.

"I see some men's underwear in there," she said, her cheeks pink when she turned to look at me.

"There's a toothbrush in the holder, along with toothpaste, men's deodorant, a razor, and Old Spice in a bag in the bathroom drawer," Veronica said as she entered the room.

I pointed to the black duffel. "And there's men's clothes here."

"Helloooo?" Mitchell's voice drifted up the stairs.

"Up here!" I called. "But we're coming back down."

We made our way back downstairs, and as soon as Mitchell came into view, he demanded, "Why didn't you lock the back door behind me?"

Instead of replying, I pressed the button on the answering machine to play the message for Mitchell. His eyebrows rose as he listened, and when the message ended, he popped the tiny cassette tape out of the machine.

"I take it that's John's voice?" He held up the tape before slipping it into the inside pocket of his jacket.

"Yes," Veronica said, "and there's a duffel bag of men's clothes in the guest room closet, and some men's toiletries in the hall bathroom."

"Where's John's car?" I asked Mitchell.

"It was parked behind the store," Mitchell said. "We took it to the station's lot. Since there wasn't an overnight bag in it, we were stumped about where he might've been staying in town until Edna told us about John and Suzanne."

"Is this house a crime scene now, since John's stuff is here?" Cynthia asked.

He held his palms up. "We don't know for sure it's John's stuff." At my incredulous look, he continued, "Yes, it's probably his, but we'll need to either find some sort of identification in or on the bag, or we'll need to check for prints."

"Well, let's go look for ID." I headed for the stairs. "I'm guessing you have some more of those little gloves with you."

"Always."

I was halfway up the stairs with Mitchell on my heels when the doorbell rang and I stumbled. Mitchell's hands grabbed my waist and steadied me before I could send us both back down the stairs.

"Whoa, there." He quickly let go of me, but his eyes held a look of concern when I glanced back at him. "You okay?"

"Yep." I smoothed my hands down my pants. "You know me —clumsy as the day is long."

Veronica's voice came to us, "You want me to answer the door?"

Mitchell turned and headed back down the few steps. "Let me. You three stay out of sight."

I sat on the steps, as I didn't have a view of the door. I assumed Veronica and Cynthia moved into the kitchen.

"Donnie," Mitchell said a few seconds later, "can I help you with something?"

I suddenly remembered Donnie Masters lived across the street from Suzanne. I wondered if Suzanne's late husband, Richard, had been friends with Donnie. They were both lawyers, so I figured they had a lot in common, though about two decades separated the two men in age. Richard was quite a bit older than Suzanne.

"I was just checking in on Suzanne." I strained to hear Donnie's voice. "I know she and John were close."

"How did you know that?" Mitchell asked.

Donnie cleared his throat. "He mentioned it when he came in to change his will." Why did he sound cagey? "Can I come in and talk to Suzanne? It's cold out here."

"She's not here."

"Is that so? Then how did you come to be inside her house? Seems like this might be an overreach of police authority."

"I gave him permission to be here." Veronica's voice was both calm and chiding. So much for her staying out of sight. "I'm always welcome in this house, and I have a key."

My jaw dropped at my pastor's wife's blatant lie, but then I realized the key was still in her pocket, so she technically did have it.

"It's also a crime scene." My jaw dropped even more at Mitchell's declaration. "So I'm going to need to ask you to leave."

Nobody said anything for several seconds. I wished I could see the look on Donnie's face.

"I don't see any crime scene tape." Donnie's voice was now belligerent.

"Haven't had time to put it up yet," Mitchell said in a conversational tone. "Just waiting for the officers to arrive."

"If I have to leave, so does she." I envisioned Donnie pointing a thick finger at Veronica.

"I don't think you get to make that decision."

"Why haven't you arrested Marty James?" Donnie demanded.

"There's some new evidence pointing in a different direction," Mitchell replied.

"What new evidence?"

"I'm not at liberty to say."

Donnie snorted loudly enough I heard it. "Of course you're not."

"But I am at liberty to say once again that you need to leave."

"What if I have some information that could help the case?"

"If that's true, why haven't you already told us this information?" Mitchell's voice had an edge to it.

"Because I just remembered it."

"Uh-huh. Spit it out, then."

"Don't you want to interview me at the station instead of here in front of *her*?"

"No, because I don't think you have anything of value to say."

I caught myself before I laughed out loud at Mitchell's statement.

"Do you find me seeing John Kemper's car leave here at around 5:20 yesterday morning to be valuable information?"

Silence descended after Donnie's declaration.

"All right." I imagined Mitchell sighed. "Let's go to the station. Mrs. Coker, do you mind waiting outside in your car until Officers Park and Pierce arrive? Make sure nobody else enters the house before then." He said this part louder, likely to ensure I heard it.

"Will do, Detective Crowe."

I stayed put until I heard everyone leave and the door close behind them. Then I made my way back down the stairs to check if Cynthia was still in the house. I found her pulling open a drawer in the kitchen.

"I'm looking for an address book," she explained and held up her gloved hand. "I put my gloves on so I don't leave fingerprints. Maybe we can find an entry in the book that says 'Aunt' something-or-other."

"Great idea. I'm gonna head upstairs to see if I can find a luggage tag on the duffel bag." I grabbed my own gloves from my coat pocket.

At that moment, Veronica entered through the back door.

"I thought Mitchell told you to wait in the car," I said as I slipped on my gloves.

"That was just because he couldn't very well leave me alone at a crime scene in Donnie's presence. I waited just long enough for them to drive out of sight."

"Ah. Cynthia's looking for an address book, and I'm headed up to see if there's a luggage tag on the bag. Come with me?"

"Sure."

"Why do you think Mitchell told Donnie this is a crime scene?" I asked as we climbed the stairs yet again.

"Probably to see the look on Donnie's face," Veronica replied, "which was smart, because he looked guilty for half a second. For a lawyer, he doesn't have a great poker face. I wouldn't want him representing me in court, that's for sure."

"Do you really think Mitchell's sending officers over here?" I asked her. If so, I probably should just leave this alone until they arrived.

"Not sure. Considering what Donnie said and what else we already found here, I'd say they're more needed at the station than here right now."

I kneeled on the floor next to the duffel and lightly ran my gloved hands along the sides, hoping to find a luggage tag. I found one hanging off the shoulder strap. It was partly stuck under the back side of the bag, and I slowly slid it out and up while grasping only the edges between my fingers.

"I guess that's proof enough," Veronica said when I flipped the tag over to reveal John's name and address.

Chapter Seventeen

"We have some updates," I told Marty fifteen minutes later as Veronica, Cynthia, and I entered his parents' house. A couple of officers had arrived at Suzanne's, and after a brief conversation, we'd left them to it.

"Let's sit at the kitchen table to talk," Henry said. "I'll get us all some drinks."

"Did you talk to Mitchell about us?" Marty asked in a low voice after the others stepped into the kitchen out of sight.

"I did." I give his bicep a squeeze. "He took it better than expected."

"Good." He gave me a quick but searing kiss, and then he nudged me into the eat-in kitchen with his hand on my lower back.

"Is your mom coming home?" I asked as I took a seat next to Marty at the solid oak table.

"She wanted to bring the kids here," he explained, "but Dad and I didn't think that was safe. Karla will be home tomorrow, and then Mom'll head back."

"We've been keeping her updated," his dad said as he poured glasses of iced tea for each of us. "Speaking of, what's the latest?"

I turned a bit in my seat so I could comfortably look at Marty.

"Suzanne wasn't home, and it looks like she's out of town. But we found evidence John stayed there Wednesday night, and he also left her a message on the answering machine on Wednesday." I explained how he was coming to town to meet with Paul. Then I relayed the conversation Mitchell had with Donnie, as well as the insights on the time of death.

"That's mostly good news for Marty, isn't it?" Henry said. "Except the time of death, that is."

"Yes," I said. "None of it is concrete evidence against anyone else, but it provides opportunity for both Paul and Donnie. We also know they both had motive, and anyone had the means, since the murder weapon came from the scene."

"True," Cynthia stated, "but the fact that the killer used an axe from the store tells us they probably didn't go there intending to kill John, right? Otherwise they would've used a weapon they brought with them for that purpose."

My stomach dropped at the logic behind what my cousin was saying. We were all silent for a few seconds while her words sank in, but then I sat up straight in my seat.

"Unless they intended to use something from the store with the purpose of framing Marty!"

"Great point, Becky." Henry took a sip of his tea.

"Beckett." Marty reached over and squeezed my thigh.

"Yeah?" I replied.

Marty said, "Just reminding Dad you want to go by your full name now."

"It's okay," I said. "I'm used to it."

"Yeah," Marty glanced from his dad to me, "but I want to make sure he calls my girlfriend by the right name."

I sucked in a breath at Marty claiming me as his girlfriend, and a smile spread across Henry's face as Cynthia's jaw dropped open.

"I hope it's okay for me to call you my girlfriend," Marty said to me.

I gave him a soft smile. "Yeah, I like hearing it."

"So do I, son." Henry was still beaming. "So do I. That's some great news in the midst of a real hard time."

Veronica watched us all with a slight grin while Cynthia smiled widely and did a little dance in her chair.

"Thanks, Dad. But let's get back to why we're all here—solving this murder before I get arrested for it. We still don't know why John was at the store so early, unless that's when and where Paul asked to meet him."

"That seems like the most logical conclusion," Veronica agreed, "but I want to know why Donnie was looking out his window so early in the morning. That seems strange. Even if you're up at that time, why would your curtains be open? It's still pitch black outside."

"What if Donnie and Paul were in on it together?" Henry mused. "Would that make any sense?"

I took a drink of my tea while I thought about the answer to that question, and everyone else seemed to also be considering whether a collaboration between the two could make sense.

"Okay," I said, "let's look at this from each man's perspective. Why would Donnie do it and get Paul involved, and vice versa?"

"We're working on the assumption that Donnie needs money due to a gambling issue," Veronica said. "So if he thought he could quietly get his hands on the money John was giving to the VFW, he could've . . . well, I was going to say he got Paul to kill John so Paul could get his inheritance, but Paul wasn't getting anything from John, so that doesn't work."

"Yeah," Marty jabbed a finger onto the tabletop, "but Paul probably didn't know about the change to the will. If Donnie wanted to use Paul to kill John, he wouldn't have told him about that, because then Paul would know he had nothing to gain financially from his dad's death."

Henry added, "But that doesn't explain why Paul would want to kill his dad. If he needed money, don't you think he would've tried to patch up his relationship with his dad instead of killing him? Then he could've asked for a loan or something."

"Maybe, maybe not." I moved my hands up and down like two sides of a scale. "We've learned this past year that killers aren't necessarily logical."

Cynthia asked, "What if Donnie told Paul about the change in the will, but Donnie convinced him that if his dad was killed and Marty was framed for it, the store wouldn't go to Marty but would go to John's kids instead? I don't think that's the way it works, but if a lawyer told me that, I'd believe them."

We all thought about that possibility for a moment.

"That makes the most sense of anything we've come up with yet," I said.

"It does," Henry said. "Great thinking, young lady."

"Thanks," Cynthia said with a proud smile.

"What about the other way around, then?" Marty asked. "What if it was Paul's idea, and he roped Donnie in somehow? What would be the story behind that?"

None of us could think of a reason Paul would try to get Donnie involved, because he likely wouldn't have known Donnie had a gambling problem and needed cash. Most people just assume lawyers are rolling in money.

Marty said, "I keep thinking to myself, 'What if it was me who'd been in the store that early?'" He shook his head and swallowed thickly, and I reached over to rub his back. "Would I have been the one who was killed?"

Henry's eyes widened. "Hold up. While I don't want to think about that, what if you *were* the intended target?"

My chest felt like it was caving in on itself at that thought, and I grasped Marty's arm.

"We need to consider that, right?" Henry asked.

I felt like I was going to throw up. I was upset enough about Marty potentially going to jail, but the thought of him being dead? I wasn't prepared for that possibility.

"Yes," Veronica said, since I couldn't speak, "that could be something to consider, but I think there was a reason John and the killer were both at the store at the same time. We now know that Paul wanted to meet John here in Cherry Hill. So doesn't it make sense that the meeting was to take place at the store at 5:30 yesterday morning?"

"That's a really strange time to meet," I was finally able to say. "Wouldn't John have been suspicious?"

"Maybe," Veronica replied, "but he wouldn't have suspected his son was going to kill him, if that's what happened. And I still want to know where Suzanne is. She didn't tell me she was going anywhere, and she obviously didn't tell John, either. I'm worried about her."

Brrrring!

Marty's dad got up to answer the phone on the kitchen wall. "Hello? … Yes, he's here. Just a minute."

He held the phone out to Marty. "It's Detective Crowe. He said he got approval from Nancy to call you."

I squeezed Marty's hand again before letting go.

He gave me a crooked smile and said quietly, "There's a phone in the living room. Why don't you go listen in?"

I hurried into the next room and picked up the phone next to Henry's recliner. I was able to stretch the cord far enough so I could see Marty in the kitchen.

"Hello?" Marty's voice came to me in stereo, both in my ear and across the fifteen feet separating us.

His eyes locked with mine, and I held my breath as I waited for Mitchell to speak.

"Marty, I have great news for you." Mitchell paused longer than I felt was necessary before continuing, "You're no longer our prime suspect, so there's not an impending arrest in your future."

My breath released in a whoosh I hoped Mitchell couldn't hear.

Marty closed his eyes and leaned against the kitchen counter. "That's a huge relief. Thanks for letting me know. Can you tell me anything else?"

"No, I'm sorry."

"How about we tell you what we've been talking about and see if that'll help you any?" I said.

"Beckett?" Mitchell said.

"Yep, I'm here, too. We've been talking, and … well, first, can you say whether Paul or Donnie is your new prime suspect?"

"No."

"Figured. Anyway, we think maybe the two of them were in on it together."

"Oh, yeah? How'd you come to that conclusion?"

I told him our theory about Donnie telling Paul about the will and suggesting he could get the store back if his dad died and Marty went to prison.

"Hmm. That's a decent theory," he admitted.

"Had you already thought about that?"

"Not that exact scenario, but we've been considering the possibility it was a group effort."

"Do you have enough to arrest Paul?" I asked.

"We don't have enough to justify it yet, especially since we didn't arrest you, Marty, with the amount of evidence we had pointing to you. That has put us in a bit of a bind, but I wouldn't change that decision even if I could."

My heart squeezed at the thought of Mitchell's integrity throughout this case.

"Did Jake and Olivia find anything else at Suzanne's?" I asked. "Is that where you found the evidence? And have you tracked her down?"

"We still don't know where Suzanne is and haven't heard from Jacqui. Barbara said she gets off work in time to be home when Parker gets home from school, though, so she should be home soon. I'm going to try her again when I get off this call. As for the other matter, Marty, can I ask you to get off the phone? You're still technically a suspect, so I shouldn't say anything directly to you, even though I know you'll hear about it."

"Sure, I'll hang up now," Marty said. "Thanks for calling."

"Yep. I'm glad we got you mostly cleared."

"I appreciate it."

Marty hung up and then came into the living room and pulled me down onto the couch next to him. I held the phone between our ears so he could hear what Mitchell said.

"He's off the other phone now," I said to Mitchell, making sure to not technically lie.

"All right. First, we checked John's keys, and there's not one matching the office key. That doesn't tell us a whole lot, though. The key could be anywhere. Second, we found a letter in John's bag from Paul, asking to meet him at the store yesterday morning at 5:30."

Marty and I looked at each other with wide eyes.

Mitchell continued, "The problem is the letter was typed, so we can't verify it actually came from Paul. There wasn't an envelope, so we're not sure if it was mailed to John or dropped off at his house or even handed to him."

"Why would you type a note like that, though?" I asked. "That seems weird. Or if you did type the message, at least you'd sign your name with a pen. I'm thinking Paul maybe didn't write it."

"Exactly, which is why we can't fully rule Marty out yet. But even if Paul didn't write it, that doesn't mean he wasn't involved in the murder."

I sighed. "This doesn't really help a whole lot, does it? The letter could've been written by Donnie or Kathleen, or even Jerry McCoy, for that matter."

"I know, which is why we're not just zeroing in on Paul. It can be difficult to pull fingerprints from paper, but Olivia is working on it as we speak. I'd guess the person who sent the letter wore gloves, though, and we'll only find John's prints."

Marty nudged me and mouthed something about Donnie looking out the window.

I nodded at him and said to Mitchell, "I also don't understand why Donnie was awake and looking out his window so early in the morning. That makes no sense unless he knew to look out the window at the time."

"You're not wrong."

"Is Donnie still there at the station?"

"No, we had no reason to keep him here."

I gripped the phone more tightly. "Do you know where Paul is?"

"No, so you need to stay on guard at all times. Don't be alone anywhere. And I can't believe I'm saying this, but get Marty and Kyle to stay with you again overnight. If the killer is thinking about going after anyone else, it would be you or Marty. I'll also make sure we patrol your street again on a regular basis. We'll do everything we can to keep both of you safe."

My throat closed up. "Thank you," I choked out. "I know this has to be hard for you, and I really respect the way you're handling it."

"I'd do anything to make sure you're safe and happy."

"You two are staying here until Kyle gets off work and can get himself to Beckett's house," Henry said to Marty and me after we headed back into the kitchen and told him and Veronica everything Mitchell said. "And Mrs. Coker, I don't feel comfortable with you and Cynthia leaving here without some protection. Donnie saw you at Suzanne's, and that makes me nervous." He gave Veronica an appraising look. "Does your husband own a gun?"

Veronica nodded. "Yes, a hunting rifle. He hasn't used it in a while, but he gets it out and cleans it on a regular basis."

Henry cocked his head at her. "Would he be able to shoot a person with it?"

Veronica laughed as if that was the silliest thing she'd ever heard. "Absolutely not, but I would if someone were physically threatening someone I love."

Henry chuckled. "Good enough. Now, you're welcome to stay

here as long as you'd like, but whenever you're ready to go home, I'd like to follow you there to ensure you arrive safely."

"What about *your* safety?" she asked.

"I'll take my shotgun along, just in case."

"All right." Veronica pushed up from her seat at the table. "Beckett, if you don't need me for anything else, Cynthia and I will head out. Call if you hear anything about Suzanne or if there's any more updates on the case."

I stood and hugged her, which she tolerated better than she would've a year earlier. "Will do. The same goes for you. Be careful."

"You, too. And we'll keep Cynthia safe until your parents get off work."

I hugged my cousin, and when I let go, I said, "You know, if you don't want to stay cooped up in the parsonage the rest of the day, why don't you two head to the newspaper office? Cynthia is interested in being a reporter like her sister," I explained to Veronica. "I'm sure Edna would be happy to show her the place and answer any questions. You can also fill her in on the new information we have and see if she learned anything interesting from any of the veterans."

"Yes! Yes!" Cynthia bounced up and down on her toes. "I'd love that."

"Sounds good," Veronica said as she put her coat on. I knew she wasn't Edna's biggest fan, but she and Cynthia seemed to have formed a bond today, so I wasn't surprised she agreed to my plan.

The moment the door closed and we were alone in the house, Marty pulled me onto his lap, wrapped me in his arms, and buried his face in my neck.

"I'm so relieved," he mumbled against my skin.

"Me, too." I ran my fingers through his hair and leaned my head against his. "We're not out of danger, but at least the police have something else to go on now. They'll figure it out."

He pulled his head back a little so he could look me in the

eyes. "Or you will. Will it help to talk it through again, taking into account what we've just learned?"

I shook my head. "The new evidence doesn't necessarily point to anyone in particular. I'm kind of surprised they decided to stop considering you as their top suspect, but I guess you're probably the least likely person to set John up like that and then be the one to call it in to the police."

Marty searched my eyes. "That argument could've held throughout this whole thing, though."

"Yeah, but today they're finally finding pieces of evidence that point toward someone else doing it, though not necessarily who. You never really made sense as the killer, but they didn't have anything even halfway concrete pointing to anyone else. Now they do."

Chapter Eighteen

The phone was ringing as Marty, Kyle, and I trooped into my house a couple hours later. I rushed to answer it before the machine kicked in.

"Hello?"

"Beckett, it's Mrs. ... Veronica."

I giggled at her greeting. She was still getting used to me calling her by her first name. But I'd told her if we were going to be friends, I wasn't going to stand on formality any longer.

"Well, hi, Mrs. Veronica." I smirked. "You know that's what I'm going to call you from now on, right?"

"Yes, whatever," she said in an annoyed tone. "Anyway, I just heard from Suzanne."

Before she could elaborate, I asked, "Is she okay?"

"She's fine. She got a call Wednesday afternoon that her aunt in Poplar Bluff wasn't doing well, so she drove down to see her before she passed. Which she did, by the way, yesterday morning, so Suzanne decided to stay there until the funeral."

My heart went out to Suzanne. That had to be hard, but I was glad she'd gotten to see her aunt before she died. Sadly, she'd also lost John around the same time.

I covered the mouthpiece and whispered to a concerned Marty

and Kyle, "We found Suzanne. She's in Poplar Bluff for an aunt's funeral."

Marty sighed in relief, and Kyle nodded as they made themselves at home in the kitchen.

Veronica continued, "In her rush, she didn't take the time to tell anyone other than Jacqui she was leaving town. She asked Jacqui to call and let me know she was leaving and might not be back for church on Sunday. As we know, Jacqui failed to do so. That girl." I could imagine Veronica shaking her head in disgust. She didn't care for the way Jacqui took advantage of her mother's generosity while giving nothing in return.

As Marty poured us all some lemonade from the pitcher in the fridge, I asked Veronica, "So why did she call now? Did Jacqui finally think it might be important to tell her mother about John?"

I watched Kyle poke around in the fridge and freezer as Veronica answered, "Jacqui didn't know John had died until Parker came home from school talking about it today. She called the police first, since she had the message from them and was obviously wondering why they needed to get in touch with her, and then she called Suzanne, who called Mitchell. Her next call was to me, and here I am."

Kyle pulled the electric skillet out of the cabinet next to the stove and plugged it in. I briefly wondered what he was doing, but if a man wanted to cook something in my kitchen, I wasn't going to stop him.

"Is she doing okay with the news of John's death?" I asked.

"She was pretty upset, but you know Suzanne. She's a strong woman. She'll be all right in the long run."

"Yes. Did she tell you anything that might be helpful?"

"As a matter of fact, she did." My friend actually sounded excited, which was rare.

"And … ?"

Marty and Kyle both turned to me with expectant looks, and I held up a finger to tell them to wait.

"When she was on her way to Poplar Bluff on Wednesday, she saw Kathleen getting gas at a station in Taylorville!"

"What?" I practically screeched, startling the men. "Is she sure?"

"Yes. Kathleen drives a blue Volkswagen bug, so she was easy to spot."

I nodded, remembering the car parked in my driveway this morning when Kathleen stopped by."You're right. You can't miss that car. I'm surprised nobody else saw her. Hold on a sec," I said to her, "I need to tell the guys this."

I relayed the info to Marty and Kyle. Kyle pumped his fist, but Marty merely looked sad. He didn't want Kathleen to be the killer any more than I did, even if that meant he was off the hook.

"What are you making over there?" I asked Kyle before getting back to Veronica.

"Spaghetti. That all right with you?"

"It's great. Thanks!"

"I see a career as a house husband in your future. Olivia better lock you down," Marty teased his roommate, who beamed and bowed, not offended in the least.

"There's more," Veronica said when I got back to her. "I asked Suzanne who Kathleen would've left the kids with while she was up here, since her husband is in Texas and John was here. She said Kathleen often left the kids home overnight with a teenage babysitter. John didn't like it, and he told Kathleen he'd watch them if she needed a break, but she insisted on getting a sitter, so his hands were tied."

"So having an overnight sitter is how she did it," I said for the guys' benefit, "*if* she did it, and we don't know that yet. But why else would she have been in the area on Wednesday? I wonder if the kids are with that sitter again, since Kathleen is here. Well, at least she was in town yesterday talking to the police, and she was here again this morning. She might not still be here."

"Suzanne said she was going to try calling Kathleen's house to see if anyone answered. I told her to call the police back and tell them everything about the sitter, since it hadn't come up in their first conversation. She also told me Kathleen and her dad had a pretty big disagreement a few weeks ago. It was partly about the kids, but also about Kathleen spending money she didn't have. She's in deep debt and kept asking him for loans, and he finally cut her off."

"So she has motive," I mused. "She needed money, and she was angry with her dad. Kathleen could've sent the letter, likely knowing exactly what to say to get her dad to agree to meet with his estranged son. He'd be especially open to mending that relationship, if things had also gone south with Kathleen last week. I can't imagine how it would feel to be on the outs with both of your kids at the same time. That might also be why John changed the will, since that happened a few weeks ago, too. Did Suzanne know about the will?"

"I didn't think to ask her," Veronica answered.

"We can't forget that Paul also has motive." Kyle waved a wooden spoon in the air. I asked Veronica to hold on while he continued, "And he could've sent that typed letter, with the express purpose of trying to frame our good buddy here." He pointed the spoon at Marty. "We know Paul was trying to get money because of what he did at the bank this morning. I still think it might be him—or Paul and Donnie in cahoots. Kathleen could've been up here Wednesday for a completely unrelated reason."

I relayed all that information to Veronica, who agreed.

"Or maybe all three of them were in on it together," I said. "Who knows? Donnie could've gotten them both involved separately, hoping at least one of them would come through."

"If Kathleen's car is so recognizable," Kyle said as he stirred the meat browning in the skillet, "why didn't anyone see it around town yesterday morning? Five thirty is pretty early, but there are plenty of people up and about at that time, and the hardware store is smack dab in the middle of town. She would've had to drive past a lot of houses and even a few vehicles on the road."

Again, I told Veronica what he said.

"Maybe Kathleen borrowed a car from someone in Taylorville," she guessed.

"Yeah, but if she borrowed a car, wouldn't that person now be suspicious about it?" I asked. "I know I would be."

"Hold on." Marty turned from where he was getting plates out of the cabinet. "Jeff's brother lives in Taylorville. He seems like a decent guy, but what if he's still secretly in love with Kathleen and let her borrow a vehicle, maybe not knowing what she was planning?"

"And he can't go to the police," I added, "for fear he'll be considered an accomplice!"

"Who?" Veronica demanded in my ear. "Who could be an accomplice?"

"Jamie Jenkins—Jeff's older brother. He dated Kathleen in high school and thought they'd get married, but she turned down his proposal after graduation. Marty thinks maybe he helped her by loaning her a car, not knowing what her intentions were."

"That's an interesting theory," Veronica replied. "I think you need to call Mitchell and tell him our thoughts on all this. And if you want to call Suzanne and speak with her directly, she gave me a number where you can reach her. I need to get off the phone and finish getting dinner ready for Harold. Call me later with any updates."

"Hold on a sec. Did you and Cynthia go by the newspaper office? And is she back with my parents now?"

"Oh! I'd already forgotten. Yes, we stopped by to see Edna. A couple of the men she talked to said they suspected something was off with the VFW books. However, when one of them questioned Donnie on it, he had a reasonable explanation for it, so they let it go."

"Interesting."

"Isn't it? Also, your dad picked Cynthia up on his way home from work."

"Good, I'm glad she's safely back with my parents."

Veronica then gave me the number where Suzanne was staying, and I immediately dialed it after hanging up the phone. Suzanne answered after the first ring. We spent a few minutes talking about John, but then she was ready to get down to business.

"Beckett, we've got to figure this out," she said. "We can't let someone get away with my John's murder!"

"We're working on it. I've got Marty and Kyle here now, and we have a few more questions for you beyond what you told Veronica. First, did you know that John changed the will?"

"I knew he met with Donnie a few weeks ago, but I didn't pry about what the meeting was about." That was surprising, as prying was one of Suzanne's favorite pastimes. "I just figured it was something to do with the store. I'll tell you, though, that I don't trust Donnie Masters any farther than I could throw him. I wouldn't be surprised if he's mixed up in this somehow."

"It seems like nobody knew about the will other than Donnie. You know," I said, "I keep wondering why John left twenty-five grand to the VFW. Does that seem strange to you? Kathleen was shocked by the amount. She said her dad didn't like talking about his time in the service, and she didn't think he was involved in the VFW."

"He *wasn't* involved," Marty said from across the table. "And I never heard him talk about the war, either."

I relayed that information to Suzanne, who agreed. "Same here," she said. "That makes the amount very suspicious. John would've had his own copy of the will. We need to find that and compare it to the will Donnie gave the police."

"I'll suggest that to Mitchell," I said. "With the three people closest to John saying they're surprised by that bequest, they'll want to look into it."

"They'd better!"

"They will. Moving on," I said, "we're all trying to figure out how Kathleen might've driven through town yesterday morning and even parked her car downtown without anyone spotting it. Nobody in town drives a blue slug bug, so it would've stood out. Do you have any thoughts on that?" I decided to let her think about it for a minute before telling her our theory.

"Well, she was in Taylorville. Maybe she has a friend there that she stayed with overnight and then used their car to drive to Cherry Hill. It was early enough they might not have even known she was gone."

"What are your thoughts on that friend being Jamie Jenkins?"

She sucked in an audible breath. "I think that's highly possible. John told me she asked him about Jamie not long ago. He wondered if she had thoughts of getting back together with him, now that she's getting divorced."

"All right. I'll tell Mitchell that. I'm planning to call him next. Is there anything else you can think of that might help?"

"No, but I'll keep wracking my brain."

"Good to know. I'm gonna let you go so I can call the police station. I'm so sorry about John, Suzanne. He was a good man."

Suzanne sniffled. "He sure was. Now go find his killer."

Chapter Nineteen

A s soon as I hung up with Suzanne, I rang the police station. Since it was past five, Barbara was off duty at the front desk, but Olivia answered.

"Is everything okay at your house?" she asked in a rush after I identified myself. "You're safe? And Marty ... and Kyle?"

I grinned and snuck a glance at Kyle, who was listening intently while finishing up the spaghetti, though I didn't know if that was because of Olivia or because he was simply curious about what I might find out.

"We're all fine. Sorry I worried you. Anyway, is Mitchell there? Can I talk to him?"

"He's not here. In fact, I'm the only one holding down the fort right now. Everybody else is out chasing down leads, but somebody had to stay here and answer the phone in case somebody calls in another tip."

"I've got several tips for you." I then told her our various theories, and she promised to pass everything on to Mitchell.

Then Olivia lowered her voice and said, "I shouldn't tell you this, but Jake and Frank are on their way to Springfield to Kathleen's house. We need to figure out if she really was home all night, or if she left the kids with the sitter. We're thinking the sitter is still there with the kids but was told not to answer the phone. They're also going to search John's house again. Jake and I went down there yesterday and didn't find anything, but we didn't really know what to look for. Now that we know about the letter, they're going to look for an envelope. And if the sitter isn't at Kathleen's house, maybe John has her number written down somewhere. It's a long shot, but we're doing everything we can think of to get to the bottom of it."

"That sounds like a good plan. Thanks for letting me know. Is there any way to get in touch with the guys and ask them to look for John's copy of the will?"

"I'll see what I can figure out," she said. "Thanks for all the info."

I hung up the phone as the men were putting the food on the table. In addition to the spaghetti, they'd also put together a salad.

"I could get used to this," I said. "Thanks, guys."

"No problemo," Kyle said. "Want me to say grace?"

That was a question I never thought I'd hear out of Kyle Korte's mouth, but it made me smile. "Go for it."

When he finished, I filled them in on what Olivia told me about Frank and Jake going to Springfield.

"If nobody's free to follow up on our theory about Jamie," Kyle said, "I'm thinking we need to take ourselves on a little trip to Taylorville to help speed things along. Either of you know where Jamie lives?"

"Why don't we just call him?" Marty asked as he twirled his fork in his spaghetti. "Wouldn't that be the safer option?"

"Element of surprise, my man." Kyle jabbed his fork in the air. "Don't want to tip them off and give Kathleen time to get away if she's there. We'll take my gun with us, just in case there's trouble."

"I think we need to call Jeff first," I said. "We can't just go off and accuse his brother of aiding and abetting a murderer behind

143

Jeff's back, not after everything that happened last year. He doesn't need to be blindsided if it turns out we're right."

Kyle pursed his lips as he assessed me. "You sure he won't tip Jamie off?"

"No, but I think that's a chance we need to take. We owe this to Jeff."

"I agree," Marty said. "But why don't you ask him to come over here, and then we'll tell him? It'd be awkward for him to call Jamie from here, and we can ask him to go with us if he wants. It might be good to have him along, if things get tense with Jamie."

"Sounds like a plan." I stood and grabbed the phone. "If he's home, he should be able to get here by the time we finish eating."

Jeff hadn't eaten dinner when he arrived less than ten minutes later, and thankfully we had enough spaghetti left for him. As he ate, we quickly filled him in on everything we'd learned throughout the day, without divulging we suspected his brother of possibly helping Kathleen. The guys and I had discussed it before Jeff arrived, and we decided I should be the one to break that news to him.

"So it could be Paul or Kathleen or Donnie, or even all three of them?" he asked. "That's great for Marty, right?"

"Yes. The focus is finally off him, even though there's no clear front-runner in the suspect race."

"I appreciate you filling me in and feeding me dinner," Jeff said, "but why am I here? Why couldn't you have told me all this over the phone?"

I took a deep breath. "What I'm going to say next might be upsetting for you, but I want you to really think about whether it could be possible."

Jeff's fork stopped halfway to his mouth, and he set it back down on his plate as he glanced between the rest of us. "I have no idea where you're going with this, but I promise to do my best to think rationally about whatever you're going to say."

"We think Kathleen might've stayed somewhere in the area with a friend Wednesday night and possibly borrowed their car—knowingly or unknowingly—early Thursday morning to come to Cherry Hill. There's no way she could've come here in her own car and not been noticed. Is there a possibility she might've stayed with your brother?"

Jeff's jaw tensed, but to his credit, he didn't immediately go on the defensive for his brother. He took a drink of iced tea while he considered what I'd said.

"Like I told you earlier," he said, "I don't think Jamie ever got over Kathleen, so it's possible she spent the night with him. But I can't see him letting her borrow his pickup without knowing why she needed it, since she had her own car. And even if she took his truck without his permission, I don't see how he wouldn't have put two and two together and called the cops once he heard about John."

Kyle pressed a hand over his heart. "People do crazy things for love. And they tend to believe the people they love. Kathleen might've convinced him she had nothing to do with it, especially with all the evidence pointing toward someone else." He nodded at Marty. "On the other hand, she could've told him he'd get in trouble if he went to the police. Accessory to murder, or whatever. Maybe she's blackmailing him with something else. Who knows?"

"I don't know, guys." Jeff looked sad now. "I don't want to think my brother would help cover up a murder." He dropped his head and closed his eyes. "Why is this happening again?"

I covered Jeff's hand with my own. "I don't know, and I know it's hard. I really hope we're wrong about this, but we plan to go to Jamie's house and talk to him and see if Kathleen's there," I said. "Even if he had nothing to do with it, he might've talked to Kathleen recently and could maybe give us some insights into

145

what's been going on with her. The police aren't available to look into it right now, so we're taking it upon ourselves to do so."

Jeff lifted an eyebrow. "You think that's safe?" He had reason to ask that question, as he was involved in a frightening confrontation with a murderer last year, along with Kyle and me.

"There's three of us—four, if you want to tag along." Kyle pointed at Jeff. "We'll have them outnumbered, and I've got my gun if we need protection. We won't be in the position we were last time. We'll be going in eyes wide open and have the upper hand, if they don't know we're coming. And no, I don't intend to or *want* to shoot anyone, though I will if it'll save someone's life. The gun is only for self-defense."

Jeff sighed and sifted his fingers through his hair. "I don't really want to go, but I think I need to, considering it's my brother. He'll be more likely to tell me what's really going on than to tell you three. No offense."

"None taken," the rest of us said in unison, and then we all laughed, though there was nothing funny about what we were about to do.

"Should we tell someone what we're planning to do?" Jeff asked. "Like the police, perhaps?"

I shook my head. "They'd just tell us to stay out of it. But if your brother was involved in some way, I think it'll be better if you talk to him before they do and maybe help him see reason before he makes things any worse."

"I think you should tell Mrs. Coker," Marty said to me as he stood and started stacking our dirty plates. "She's kind of your partner in … well, I was going to say crime, but I guess more accurately, she's your partner in solving crimes. I don't think she needs to go with us, but she'd feel left out if you didn't at least tell her our plans. Plus, she can be the person who actually does call the cops if she doesn't hear from us in a certain amount of time."

"Good idea."

Chapter Twenty

"Why did I not call shotgun?" Kyle whined. "Of all times for me to forget, it's when it means I have to fold myself up like a pretzel in the back of your tiny car."

He was talking about my Pinto, which was plenty big enough for just me but a tight squeeze for me plus three grown men. Since the three of them each drove pickup trucks that only seat three, we were forced to take my car. Marty claimed my keys and Jeff called shotgun before Kyle realized the situation, so he was stuck with me in the minuscule backseat of my two-door car. It was quite entertaining watching him climb in.

"At least let me pick the radio station," Kyle wheedled as Marty fired up the car and Jeff stowed Kyle's unloaded handgun in the glove box. "It's the least you can do."

"Fine." Marty turned the radio dial without needing to ask what channel his roommate wanted and landed on Y107.

Kyle immediately began singing along to "We Built This City" at the top of his lungs. Jeff turned to give him a pointed look as he turned the volume down. Kyle toned it down a little, but not fully. I grinned at his enthusiasm and joined him as we drove through town.

When the song ended, Marty turned the volume down so we

could barely hear it. "Beckett, what's our plan for when we get there?"

"First, we'll see if Kathleen's car is parked outside. Jeff, does your brother's house have a garage?"

He twisted around to look back at me. "Yeah, a one-car, but his pickup is jacked up too high to fit in it, so the garage is more of a storage space."

"Is there enough room to get Kathleen's car in there, do you think?"

"Sure, if they moved some stuff around."

"So even if we don't see her car, she could be there. That means we have to be prepared for anything."

"Which means what?" Kyle asked.

"I think if we can see her car," Marty said, "we go find a payphone, call the police, and then go back and park down the street to make sure she doesn't leave while we wait for them to come." He looked at me in the rearview mirror. "They will come, right?"

"I'd think so. I'm sure they want to talk to her now that they know she was in the area. Maybe they'd just call? But we'd still be able to watch and see if she leaves and then follow her."

"Kathleen's not the only one with a noticeable car," Kyle said. "She'd spot this thing following her in five seconds, even in the dark. It's brighter than the moon."

"True," I replied. "I guess we'll cross that bridge if we come to it. If we can't tell whether she's there, we'll just go to the door."

Marty asked, "And what's our reason for being there? I don't think we thought this through well enough. If Jamie sees the four of us standing on his porch and he's involved in some way, he's gonna know something's up and slam the door in our faces."

"I got it!" Kyle raised his hand and jammed it on the roof of the car. "Ouch!" He cradled his hand against his chest like it was a baby. "This car is the size of a ... a ... I don't know what, but something really small!"

Jeff chuckled. "Get it together, man, and tell us your idea."

"All right, so you," he poked Jeff's shoulder with his good hand, "and you," he tapped my knee, "are going to pretend you're on a date. Let's say you've been to Jefferson City for dinner. On the way home, you've gotta pee really bad, Beckett, so Jeff decides to stop by his brother's house so you don't have to use a nasty gas station bathroom." He grinned proudly. "How's that for an excellent idea?"

Marty caught my eye in the rearview mirror again and I gave him a smile and a small nod. He asked, "What if I don't want my girlfriend to pretend she's on a date with someone else?"

The car was silent for several seconds except for the low sound of Stevie Wonder singing "Part-Time Lover" on the radio.

"Excuse me?" Kyle said incredulously. "I've been with you two for more than an hour tonight, *and I even cooked you dinner,* and you didn't find it important to fill me in on this juicy little piece of gossip?"

"We were a little preoccupied trying to solve a murder." I squeezed his arm. "Sorry." I realized in that moment I hadn't told Trixie about my decision, either. I needed to do that as soon as I got home, regardless of the hour.

"I guess congratulations are in order, then," Jeff said. "While I like Mitchell, I like Marty a lot better." He gave his friend a playful punch on the arm. "Glad to hear you're planning to stick around Cherry Hill, Beckett, even if that means you've gotta put up with this guy." He shot me a grin over his shoulder.

"Yes, yes, it's all great," Kyle said. "We're all happy. Well, I'd be happier if you'd told me an hour ago, but whatever. Congrats to the lovebirds. Anyway, Marty, if you have a problem with my plan, I can come up with another one."

"No, I think it's a great idea," Marty said. "Beckett was Jeff's high school girlfriend, and Kathleen was Jamie's high school girlfriend. It's a great way for them to lead into talking about Kathleen, whether she's there or not."

"But how do we explain you two being in the car?" Jeff asked. "I don't think we'd take you on a date with us."

"You can let us out down the street," Kyle said in a matter-of-fact tone.

"Yeah, because there's nothing suspicious about two men standing on the side of a residential street in the dark," Marty replied.

"I didn't say my plan was perfect!" Kyle retorted.

"All right," I said in a calming voice. "Let's think this through. Jeff, you know the street. Are there any streetlights? Hills? Curves? Would we be able to drop these two off a block or so away and it not be conspicuous if anyone saw them walking down the street after dark? Would they be able to stay mostly hidden behind trees or shrubs or anything? We'd want them to be able to get to the house for backup if we need it."

Jeff nodded. "Yeah, that shouldn't be a problem. There's plenty of trees and stuff. No clue about streetlights, though."

"We'll drop them off, then," I said. "And I think once you and I get inside and see whether Kathleen is there and how Jamie reacts to us being there, we'll just have to wing it."

"Beckett, you'll need to actually go into the bathroom, though, to sell it," Kyle said. "That'll leave Jeff by himself and you'll be out of his sight. Is that okay with both of you? I don't love that idea myself."

"I don't like it, either," Marty added.

"We should be fine as long as we don't bring up anything about the murder or Kathleen until I come back from the bathroom," I said.

"Yeah, but if Kathleen is there, won't she be suspicious of you being on a date instead of trying to solve the murder and keep Marty out of jail?"

"She also saw me at your house this morning," Marty said, "which would make her wonder why you're on a date with Jeff tonight."

I replied, "When I talked to her at The Check, I told her you and I were just friends. Which we were at the time."

"And now you're looooooovers!" Kyle sing-songed.

"Um, no," I said. "Please don't ever call us that again."

Kyle saluted me. "Gotcha. One more thing. Jeff, you're taking my gun. You don't have to use it or even load it if you don't want to, but will you be able to pretend you might shoot someone, if it comes to that? Even if it's your brother you have to aim at?"

Jeff's shoulders rose as he took a deep breath. "Yeah, I can do that if it means keeping Beckett safe."

"And keeping *you* safe," Marty added. "We don't want you being a martyr in there."

Jeff nodded. "Let's keep the gun loaded, just in case."

"You ready for this?" Jeff asked me on his brother's front porch. The light wasn't on, so I could barely make out his face.

After making one pass by the house to check for any sign of Kathleen's car, we'd dropped Marty and Kyle off just out of sight around the corner. Surprisingly, Marty kissed me in front of the other guys before I got into the driver's seat. Not that I was complaining.

Jeff and I waited in the car in the driveway long enough to give the other guys time to get down the street and hide behind the bushes in the yard next door. The street had no streetlights, so they wouldn't have much trouble staying out of sight.

"Not really," I replied, "but we're here, so let's do this."

Jeff pressed the doorbell, and we heard it ring inside. We looked at each other when we heard footsteps, but it took about thirty seconds for the door to swing open, revealing Jamie Jenkins wearing nothing but a pair of sweatpants, his slight beer belly on full display.

"Jeff," he said with a frown, "what're you doing here?" He peered at me. "Becky Monahan? Is that you?"

I bounced from foot to foot. "Yep, it's me. Great to see you again. We hate to bother you, but Jeff and I are on our way home from dinner, and I really gotta go to the bathroom. I didn't think I could make it all the way home, so Jeff suggested we stop here instead of a gas station. You know how gross those bathrooms can be. Anyway, I hope you don't mind." I shot him a pained smile and even crossed one leg over the other to emphasize my need.

Jamie opened the door wide. "Come on in. Bathroom's down the hall. First door on the left."

"Thank you!" I said as I sped by him, offering up a silent prayer that nothing bad would happen in the minute I'd need to spend in the bathroom before I could reasonably come back out.

I closed and locked the bathroom door behind me, and then I actually did use the facilities. The walls were thin enough I could hear the guys talking, so they could likely hear what I was doing, too. Embarrassing as that was, I needed to keep up the ruse as well as possible.

When I exited the bathroom, I noticed one of the other doors off the hallway was closed, and I was pretty sure it had been open before. I wondered if Kathleen was hiding behind that door, but I didn't think it was wise to check, so I rejoined the men in the living room. A quick scan of the room revealed the front door wasn't fully closed, and I wondered if that was Jeff's way of giving the other guys a way to potentially hear what was happening inside the house as well as easily enter if needed. The other observation of note was a pink cardigan draped over the back of a kitchen chair in the adjoining room.

The brothers were talking about Cherry Hill High's upcoming basketball game against Taylorville. They seemed at ease with each other, but when I appeared, Jamie took a few steps toward the door, signaling he wasn't up for any more conversation. I needed to speak up, and fast.

"Jamie, I talked to Kathleen Kemper this morning." I purposely didn't use her married name when mentioning her. "You dated her in high school, right? It's so sad what happened to her dad."

Jamie's eyes darted toward the hallway and back to me. It took all my strength to not look at Jeff, but I didn't want to tip Jamie off yet. I wondered if I should somehow alert Marty and Kyle to Kathleen's potential presence in the house.

"Yeah." Jamie crossed his arms over his chest. While I was in the bathroom, he had thankfully put on a T-shirt. "It's a real shame. John was a good man." He couldn't meet my gaze, and he glanced toward the hallway yet again.

"He was," I agreed, not budging from my spot even though Jamie took another step toward the door. "Have you talked to Kathleen recently? Do you still keep in touch?"

Jamie shot me a narrowed look before continuing to the door and opening it wide. "No." He didn't elaborate, but I could tell he was lying. He obviously wasn't going to give us any more information about Kathleen, so there was no point in staying or accusing him of anything. I didn't think he suspected we thought she was in his house. Therefore our best course of action would be to leave and keep an eye on the house.

I looked at Jeff and nodded toward the door. "Ready to go?" I thanked Jamie for letting me use his bathroom, the brothers said goodbye, and within seconds we were back on the porch with the door closed behind us.

Jeff nudged me off the porch ahead of him. "What now?" he asked in a low voice.

"We'll talk in the car."

The bushes next door moved slightly, alerting us to the other guys' presence. I handed Jeff the keys, as I'd need to get back into the backseat when Marty and Kyle joined us in a minute. He backed us out of the driveway and then slowly drove down the street and around the corner out of sight of Jamie's house. Within thirty seconds, the others arrived and joined us in the car. This time, Kyle made Marty sit in the back with me, which my boyfriend didn't complain about, since he didn't mind being squished into a confined space with me. Jeff turned off the headlights and made a U-turn so we could turn back onto Jamie's street and park along the curb several houses down.

We filled the guys in on what happened, and they told us they were able to peek inside the garage window and could see the faint outline of a Volkswagen Beetle parked inside. Suddenly, a knock on the passenger window made me jump and Kyle screech.

"Calm down, buddy. It's Mitchell," Jeff informed us, and Kyle cranked the window down.

I could barely make out Mitchell's form in the dark. He had squatted down so he couldn't be seen from the street.

"What do you four think you're doing?" he practically hissed at us. "Do you realize how dangerous this is?"

"I've got a gun," Kyle piped up.

Mitchell sighed. "That's not exactly comforting."

"Why are you here?" I asked Mitchell.

"After you called Mrs. Coker to tell her your harebrained scheme, her husband convinced her we should know about it, so she called the station just as I arrived back there. We called Barbara back in to answer the phone, and Olivia and I raced over here. I'm glad we arrived before you did anything stupid." He craned his neck so he could look directly at me. "Please tell me you haven't done anything stupid."

"Wellllll …"

His jaw tensed. "Beckett—"

"Hey," Marty said in a stern voice, "cut her some slack. We had a good plan and a cover story, and Jeff was there with Kyle's gun to keep her safe."

"Fine." Mitchell huffed out a breath. "Somebody tell me what happened, and fast."

I quickly gave him a rundown of our encounter with Jamie, and Kyle told him Kathleen's car appeared to be in the garage.

"So you didn't see Kathleen, but you're pretty sure she's in the house, even though Jamie claimed he wasn't in contact with her?" Mitchell asked, seemingly for clarification.

"Yes," I replied as the guys all nodded. "What are you going to do?"

"We need to talk to both of them, so Olivia and I will go to the door and see if anyone answers. If not, we don't have a warrant, so we can't force our way in. In fact, we don't have enough cause to get a warrant. Meanwhile, you four," he made eye contact with each of us, "will go back to Cherry Hill."

I pursed my lips. "Yeah, I don't think we're gonna do that."

Mitchell sighed again. "Well, I can't force you to leave, but please don't get involved any further. I don't want any of you getting hurt. And back the car up so it can't be seen from the front door. This thing stands out like a sore thumb."

"We don't want you or Olivia getting hurt, either," Marty said, "so we're staying here for backup. You've had my back throughout this mess, and now I'm having yours. End of discussion."

The two men locked eyes for several seconds.

"Fair enough," Mitchell said. "But be careful, all of you."

"Always," I said, which resulted in a disbelieving snort from Mitchell.

Marty asked him, "Was Olivia able to get a message to Jake and Frank about looking for John's copy of the will?"

"She called the local force down in Springfield, and they were going to send an officer to try to track the guys down and get them the message." He tapped the car door. "All right, I gotta go. Be careful." Then he took off down the street behind us.

"So what's our plan now?" Jeff asked as he backed the car up about twenty yards without turning on the headlights. "If Mitchell and Olivia get inside, how will we know what's happening and if they need our help?"

"I doubt they'll need our help, since they both have guns," I said. "But I think we need to be prepared for Kathleen to slip out the back. Marty and I will sneak down there to keep watch in the backyard."

"*Jeff* and I will sneak down there," Marty said. "You should stay here, where it's safe."

I leaned over and gave him a quick peck on the lips. "While I

155

appreciate your concern for my welfare, I must respectfully decline. I'm going."

"And you're not going, Marty," Kyle said. "I'm the only one of us who I think would actually be willing to fire a gun in the vicinity of another person if needed. Plus, we don't need one suspect trying to take down another one. It won't look good for you, Marty. And Jeff, I don't want you to be involved if something crazy happens with your brother down there. It's me and Beckett, or it's nobody."

While we were arguing, a Cherry Hill police cruiser passed us and pulled into Jamie's drive.

"Time to go, boys," I said. "Whoever wants to come with me can come, but I'm going, regardless."

Chapter Twenty-One

I pushed on the back of Kyle's seat to spur him into action, and he quickly opened the door and helped me out of the backseat. He stuck his gun into the back waistband of his jeans and closed the car door quietly. Thankfully Marty and Jeff stayed put.

We made our way through the darkness and peered around the next-door bushes as Mitchell and Olivia rang the doorbell.

"Let's get to the backyard," I said under my breath, and Kyle jerked his head in that direction, signaling me to follow him. Since he'd already been here, I trusted his instincts on how to get where we needed to go without being seen.

We made it through the neighbors' side yard without alerting any people or outdoor animals to our presence. The two backyards were separated by a four-foot high chain-link fence covered in ivy. We slipped through the gate into the neighbors' yard and crouched behind the fence so we had a view of Jamie's back door. Within seconds, the door cracked open and a woman slipped outside, closing the door carefully behind her.

Kyle whispered, "Stay here," and nimbly hopped the fence.

The woman—presumably Kathleen—was tiptoeing away in the other direction, so she didn't see Kyle until he was upon her. He snuck one arm around her waist from behind while clamping his other hand over her mouth. She started to struggle, but he must have whispered something to her, because she quickly stilled in his arms. Since he had her immobilized, I awkwardly scrambled over the fence and crossed the yard to them.

Kathleen's eyes went wide when I stepped in front of her.

"If he removes his hand, are you gonna scream?" I asked.

She shook her head, and Kyle slowly moved his hand away from her mouth while keeping a firm hold on her waist.

"I didn't kill my dad," she said frantically, "I swear."

"It sure doesn't seem that way," I said.

"Please just let me explain!"

"Seems like if you wanted to explain something, you could've done so to the police officers inside the house instead of sneaking out the back door like a criminal." I chose to ignore the hypocritical fact that I was sneaking around in backyards like a criminal. "Or you could've done it yesterday."

"I'm not completely innocent," she said, "but I didn't kill him. I promise I'll tell the police everything if you'll let me go back inside."

I nodded, and Kyle removed his arm from her body but then grasped her elbow with his hand, ensuring she wouldn't try to run. When Kathleen turned toward the back door, she got a look at Kyle's face and stilled.

"You're not Jeff."

"I'm not."

"You were at The Check this morning," she stated. "Beckett pointed you out, but I can't remember your name."

"Not sure I want to remind you what it is until I'm sure you're not a murderer."

Kathleen huffed out a cynical laugh. "Fair enough. But where's Jeff?"

"Right here."

I spun toward Jeff's voice so quickly on my bad leg I lost my balance. Thankfully Marty raced forward to catch me before I teetered to the ground.

Jeff explained, "We figured we'd come make sure all was well back here."

"Yep, we're good." I swept my hand toward the back door. "We were just headed back inside so Kathleen can talk to the police."

Jeff crossed his arms over his chest and glared at Kathleen. "I can't believe you got my brother wrapped up in this."

"I'm sorry. I didn't kill my dad," she reiterated for Jeff and Marty's benefit, "but I know who did. Just let me get back in there and explain."

In response, Kyle steered her up the two steps to the back door, and we all filed in behind them.

When I caught sight of Mitchell's face, he was shaking his head with his eyes closed. I wasn't sure if he was frustrated with Kathleen, Jamie, or all of us, but it didn't matter.

"Kathleen claims to know who the killer is," I explained as Kyle led her to the couch and not-so-gently nudged her down onto it. "She also says she's not entirely innocent."

"If I ask the rest of you to leave, will you?" Mitchell asked, referring to me and the men who came with me.

"Not a chance." I narrowed my eyes at Kathleen. "If you had immediately confessed to whatever you're about to tell us, you'd have made things a lot easier for all of us, especially Marty."

She gave Marty a beseeching look. "I'm sorry. I truly am. And I wouldn't have let you go to prison for a crime you didn't commit. I tried to send Beckett down the right path with what I told her this morning. And I thought Suzanne would know why Dad was in town and tell everyone within shouting distance. I was hoping you'd figure it out before I needed to come forward." Then she swept her gaze across the rest of us. "Can we all sit down? I feel weird being the only person sitting."

"Not sure I'm inclined to make you not feel weird," Mitchell replied. "In fact, I should be taking you to the station instead of talking to you here."

"If you need to arrest me," she held her arms out in front of her, wrists together, "I get it. But I feel like Marty deserves to hear what I have to say. Plus, the sooner I talk, the sooner you can make an arrest."

"We'll see whether an arrest is warranted after I hear what you have to say."

Mitchell grabbed a chair from the kitchen table and brought it into the living room so he could sit across the coffee table from Kathleen. The rest of us also took seats in various places around the room. I ended up next to Kathleen, and Jamie claimed the spot on her other side and held her hand.

Mitchell flipped open his notebook and started to ask Kathleen a question, but then he stopped and asked Jamie, "You have a tape player and a blank tape? I'd like to record this conversation. In fact, I need to. If you don't have the equipment, we'll have to take this to the station."

Jamie looked to Kathleen, who nodded her assent.

"Be right back," he said, and he disappeared down the hallway.

A minute later he reappeared with a small boom box and a blank tape that was still in its clear plastic wrapping. Olivia quickly got everything set up to record and tested it.

"We're good to go," she declared as she hit the "record" button. "Go ahead, Detective Crowe."

Mitchell stated the date, time, location, and everyone who was present, which took a minute.

"All right, Kathleen, I'd like you to tell us who you believe killed your father, and then I want the whole story from the beginning."

Kathleen took a deep breath, and said in a shaky breath, "It was my brother and Donnie who did it." She covered her mouth with her hand as tears slipped down her cheeks.

While I couldn't say anyone in the room was surprised by her declaration, we all exchanged a mixture of excited and relieved glances. Meanwhile, Jamie handed Kathleen a tissue from a box next to the couch and then rubbed circles on her back.

"Just to be clear for the recording," Mitchell said, "you're saying Paul Kemper and Donnie Masters killed John Kemper."

"Yes. Well, I'd guess just one of them killed him, but they were both there."

"And how do you know this?"

"Because I saw them both come out the back door of the hardware store early yesterday morning acting all shady, and then I went inside and found my dad." She covered her mouth with her hand again, and I was afraid she was going to be sick.

"Let's go back to the beginning of this story, shall we?" Mitchell prompted. "Make sure to include why you were behind the hardware store before dawn and why you failed to tell us this information immediately."

"I think you all know that Dad and Paul weren't on good terms," she said, and we all nodded. "Dad was pretty upset about it, and then he and I got into it a few weeks ago about my financial situation, so that made things even worse. Then he called me Wednesday afternoon and said Paul had left a letter taped to his door. He said Paul wanted to try to work things out with him and wanted to meet him at the store at 5:30 yesterday morning. I told Dad that sounded strange, and he shouldn't go. I mean, why would Paul not just go over to Dad's house to talk to him? Why drive all this way to meet at the store so early in the morning?" She shook her head. "I wish he'd listened to me."

Mitchell said, "We found the letter, but we didn't know how it had been delivered, so you've answered that question for us." He moved his hand in a rolling motion. "Go on."

"Dad said he didn't care where Paul wanted to meet. He was just glad Paul wanted to talk to him again after all that had happened. He really hoped Paul had changed, but he obviously hadn't."

"So why did you decide to come up from Springfield?" Mitchell asked.

"I thought Paul might be up to no good, and I wanted to keep an eye on things, so I called my usual sitter for the kids, and I drove up here and spent the night with Jamie. Then I borrowed his truck to go to Cherry Hill the next morning, because Paul would've spotted my car from five miles away. I got there twenty minutes early, parked a few blocks away, walked down, and hid behind the dumpsters in the parking lot behind the store. I figured Dad and Paul would go in the back door, and I planned to sneak into the store after they went in, assuming they wouldn't lock the door behind them."

"Why didn't you just let them know you were there?" Mitchell asked, voicing my own question.

"Paul has always accused me of sticking my nose where it doesn't belong. I knew if he was aware of my presence, he'd leave. Even though I was pretty sure he wasn't there to make up with Dad, I wanted to give him the benefit of the doubt. I didn't want to mess things up and take away the opportunity for Dad to reconnect with his son, on the off chance I was wrong. And I never for one minute thought he was going to kill Dad." She sniffled again.

"Okay." Mitchell scribbled something in his notebook. "Continue."

"So Dad and Paul both showed up, and Dad used his key to let them in. I was about to leave my hiding spot when Donnie came sneaking through the lot. I have no idea why he was there or if Paul or Dad knew he was coming. I mean, I guess one of them had to tell him they were going to be there, but I don't know which one of them did. Anyway, once Donnie went inside, I chickened out and didn't go in. I didn't know how Donnie knew they'd be there or what he planned to do, and combined with not knowing what Paul was up to, I was afraid I'd get caught up in something bad." She closed her eyes again. "I wish I'd gone in. Maybe I could've done something to help Dad."

"No," Jamie said fiercely. "You probably would've gotten killed too. I keep telling you there was nothing you could've done."

"He's probably right," I added, even though Mitchell had told the rest of us to keep quiet. I placed a hand on Kathleen's arm. "Don't beat yourself up about that."

"But *you* would've gone in there," Kathleen said to me. "Heck, you waltzed right in here a little while ago, obviously suspecting I was here and was a murderer."

Mitchell shot me a stern look. "But she shouldn't have. It really wasn't a smart move."

I glared at him, and he shrugged in response.

He turned his attention back to Kathleen. "What happened next?"

"I waited there behind the dumpster, hoping and praying nothing bad was happening inside. It wasn't long before Donnie rushed back out and hustled across the parking lot in the direction he originally came from. His hands were in his coat pockets, which I noticed because it's dumb to walk with your hands in your pockets, even if it's cold and you don't have gloves. Anyway, his clothes were all dark, so I wouldn't have been able to see any blood. I thought about going into the store then, but I was still scared, so I waited for Paul to come out, which he did a couple minutes later. It was still dark out, obviously, but there's a light above the back door to the washateria next door, so I could see enough to tell there were dark stains on his khaki pants."

"Was he wearing gloves?" Mitchell asked.

Kathleen squinted while she thought about it. "Yeah, I think he was."

"All right. What did you do next?"

"I waited another minute until I was sure they weren't coming back, and I ran inside and ..." She choked back a sob.

"And you found your dad?" I asked softly. I could feel her pain to an extent, since I'd also discovered a dead body recently, though he wasn't a relative.

Kathleen nodded.

Mitchell gave her a few moments to collect herself before asking, "Did you touch him?"

"I put my hand on his back to feel if he was breathing, and he wasn't." She covered her mouth with her hand again.

"I understand how upsetting that must've been for you, but why didn't you call the police?" Mitchell asked.

"I panicked," Kathleen admitted. "I was afraid you'd think I'd done it. I mean, how else could I explain my presence there? I didn't think anyone would believe me if I told them the truth." She sighed. "On the other hand, I had no idea where my brother or Donnie had gone, and they had just killed someone! What if I told the police and you *did* believe me, but then you just sent me home, while my dad's murderers remained out in the world somewhere? I could've been their next target—or my kids could've. So I ran back to Jamie's truck, came back here to get my car, and rushed home to be with the kids. I didn't even tell Jamie what had happened. I couldn't. Not then. It was all too raw. And I'm not going to admit that I ever did tell Jamie, because he didn't do anything wrong. He has just been here to support me in my grief and my fear." She gripped his hand tightly.

"I know it was wrong to stay quiet." She balled her free hand into a fist. "I *know* it was, especially once I discovered Marty was the prime suspect. But I was scared, and I was praying one of you would figure it out without me having to tell you." She looked Marty in the eye. "I'm so sorry, Marty. It's *my* fault you had to find my dad lying on that floor. It's *my* fault everyone thought you killed him. And I'll never forgive myself for that."

Chapter Twenty-Two

"I do forgive you," Marty said quietly to Kathleen, and I thought my heart might explode with love for that man. "And it wasn't your fault. You didn't kill your dad. You didn't set me up to be the fall guy. Your brother did that. Donnie did that."

"And frankly," I added, "nobody really thought Marty was the killer. It was pretty obviously a frame-up from the beginning. It just took a little time and some digging to find evidence pointing us to the real killers."

Kathleen's nose scrunched up. "What I don't understand is why you thought it was me." Her eyes widened. "Wait. You don't still think it was me, do you?"

I glanced at Mitchell before saying, "The police maybe can't say one way or the other yet, but I don't think you did it. Everything you've told us matches up with what we already suspected about your brother and Donnie. You came into the picture when we finally got ahold of Suzanne this evening, and she told us she saw you at a gas station in Taylorville on Wednesday. And FYI, the reason she hadn't said anything about why your dad was in town is because *she* wasn't in town. She left unexpectedly Wednesday afternoon to go see a dying aunt in Poplar Bluff. Anyway, she also told us you sometimes left the kids home overnight with a sitter, and she mentioned you'd asked your dad about Jamie recently. We also didn't know for sure who wrote that letter, because it was typed, so there was no handwriting to compare. Put that all together, and it really looked like you were the killer."

"Yeah, I can see how you'd think that," Kathleen said. "But hopefully my explanation confirms I didn't actually do it. The problem is even though you now have a witness of sorts, you still don't know which of the two men actually killed my dad. And beyond that, there's still no actual proof against either of them."

"Thanks to your account, we have enough to bring both of them in, if we can find them," Mitchell said. "We found a couple sets of fingerprints on the letter. One will be your dad's, and we'll see if the other matches up with your brother or Donnie. We'll also need to take your prints just to officially rule you out. We can do that before we leave. Two officers are on their way to your dad's house now to look for the envelope, in case that has any clues." He glanced at his watch. "Actually, they're probably there now. They were also planning to go to your house to see if you were there or if your kids were with a sitter who could possibly verify whether you were home overnight on Wednesday. What I'd like to know is where your kids are now. Are they somewhere safe?"

Kathleen nodded. "They're with a friend in Springfield. They don't know about their grandpa yet." Another tear rolled down her face, and she wiped it away. "I knew I'd need to spend at least a few days here while you were investigating. I didn't think we'd be in any danger from Paul or Donnie, since I hadn't spoken up yet, but I didn't want to take any chances by bringing the kids here with me. And I didn't dream anyone would think I'd be staying with Jamie. We've been careful not to leave my car parked outside."

"That's good. Until we catch up with Paul and Donnie, don't tell anyone else where you or your kids are."

"Okay." Kathleen bit the inside of her cheek. "Are you going to arrest me?"

We all focused on Mitchell, waiting for his verdict.

"I could charge you with obstruction of justice," he said, "but it probably won't stick. Thinking back on what you've said in our official conversations with you, I don't think you outright lied about anything. You just avoided telling the entire truth not because you were protecting the killers but because you were protecting yourself and your kids. So for now, I'm not taking you in. I suggest you stay here with Jamie, where you should still be relatively safe. None of us," he gave each of us a stern look, "will tell a soul outside the police department where you are or what you've told us. Just don't leave the area unless you need to go see your kids. In that case, let us know where you're going."

"I can't believe Mitchell wouldn't tell us what he's planning to do next," I complained to the guys as we drove back to Cherry Hill.

"You did your part." Marty's hand landed on my thigh and squeezed. "You helped get things to this point, and now the police know who they're going after. The best thing for us to do is stay out of it and let them finish this out. I'm not going to tell you what to do, but I'd really prefer you let the police do their jobs this time without putting yourself into any more danger."

I sagged against him and leaned my head on his shoulder. "I just want to help."

"I know you do, and you're great at that. But Mitchell is also great at his job, so let's allow him to do it, yeah?"

"For the record," Kyle said, "I second Marty's opinion on this."

Jeff raised his hand. "And I third it. I don't want to be staring down the barrel of another gun ever in my life, and I don't think Kyle does either. Once was enough. But if you take it upon yourself to try to go after Paul and Donnie, we're all going to feel the need to tag along. I'm asking you to not put us in that position."

Kyle pointed his thumb toward Jeff. "What he said."

Marty squeezed my thigh again but didn't say any more.

I placed my hand on top of his. "Okay, I promise I won't go after Paul or Donnie."

"Or anyone else," Jeff clarified, knowing I could be leaving myself a loophole.

"Or anyone else. You guys have all been through the wringer this past year, and I don't want to add to that. You were troopers today, and I appreciate you going with me to Kathleen's. I shouldn't have asked you to do that."

"You didn't ask," Kyle said. "And I, for one, was honored to go and be your sidekick. The adrenaline was running high when we decided Kathleen was the main suspect and we should try to find her, and I wanted to go along. But I'd rather not repeat the experience. Kathleen shoved a pointy elbow in my gut before I assured her I wasn't planning to hurt her. That's as much of an injury as I'd like to get."

I reached up and clasped his shoulder. "I'm so sorry, Kyle."

"Not directly your fault, but thanks all the same."

"Now that we've decided on no further involvement in this case," Jeff tapped his fingers in a drumroll on the steering wheel, "let's talk about how Kyle couldn't keep his eyes off Officer Pierce back there at Jamie's house."

Kyle crossed his arms over his chest, and I giggled.

"I don't want to talk about it," Kyle declared.

"Yeah, right," Marty said. "When have you ever shied away from talking about a woman?"

"Okay, fine," Kyle gave in quickly. "Let's talk about her. Was she looking at me when I wasn't looking at her?"

Marty laughed. "*Was* there a time you weren't looking at her with your puppy dog eyes?"

"I did not have puppy dog eyes!"

"You kinda did," Jeff said. "Now tell us everything."

Kyle sighed happily. "She's awesome." He turned to look at me. "Do you think she'd go to the movies with me? I want to take her to see *Murphy's Romance* before it leaves the theater in Taylorville."

"I think she would," I said.

"You'll never know if you don't ask," Marty added.

"All right. I'll do it." He then spent the rest of the drive home telling us all about Olivia. I was glad for the distraction from the case and the reality that the murderer was still out in the world somewhere. I was also happy my friend seemed to have finally set his sights on a good woman who appeared to like him back.

We were all laughing at something Kyle said when we filed into my house via the door from the garage. A movement to my left caught my eye, and when I turned my head toward a chair at the kitchen table that hadn't been visible from the door, I stopped in my tracks. Marty bumped into me, Jeff bumped into him, and Kyle then added to the forward movement. Thankfully Marty caught me—once again—and none of us fell.

"Oomph!" Kyle exclaimed. "Why'd you stop?"

I pointed at the table, and the three guys turned to look at Paul Kemper, who we'd apparently roused from a nap at my kitchen table. A handgun lay on the table next to him, and he scrambled for it.

Kyle whipped his gun out of the waistband of his jeans before I could blink, and Marty shoved me behind him. He then quickly backed us toward the entrance to the living room and pushed me out of sight as soon as we cleared the threshold.

"Don't even think about firing that gun," I heard Kyle say.

I wanted to peek around the corner, but Marty kept a hand on my shoulder, holding me out of sight.

"Get down on the floor," he hissed at me.

I thought about arguing for half a second, but then I decided

I'd rather not get shot, so I dropped to my hands and knees. But instead of staying still, I crawled over to the stereo, shoved a tape into the tape deck, and punched the record button. I wasn't sure it would catch the conversation from the next room, but I figured I might as well try. We'd caught another killer's confession in a similar fashion.

As I crawled back toward Marty, Paul said to Kyle, "And don't you think about firing yours."

"I need everyone else to leave," Kyle ordered in an eerily calm voice.

Marty didn't move, and it didn't sound like Jeff did either. I lay flat on the ground with my head near the kitchen but not close enough for Paul to be able to see me. Nobody was going to leave Kyle alone with a killer.

"Somebody call the police, then," Kyle said.

"I've got it," Jeff said.

"No," Kyle shouted, and I tensed in response because I couldn't see what was happening. "You keep that gun pointed at me, you hear me?"

Paul must've complied, because Kyle said, "That's right. Go ahead and make that call, Jeff. Now, Paul, how'd you get in here?"

Paul replied, "The back door lock was easy to pick. She really should have a deadbolt that doesn't have a keyhole on the outside. Dumb move."

"Beckett is the farthest thing from dumb," Kyle nearly growled. "You shut up."

"Actually," I yelled from my spot on the ground, "don't shut up. I want to know why you're here."

Jeff started talking on the phone in the kitchen at that moment, so we had to wait to hear what Paul had to say for himself. It didn't take Jeff long to tell the person on the other end of the line what was happening. After he finished speaking, he listened to something the other person said for several seconds before hanging up.

"They're on the way," he stated unnecessarily.

I said loudly, "Answer my question, Paul. And say it loud enough for me to hear you clearly so I don't have to repeat myself." I wanted to hear what he had to say before Mitchell took him away, and I needed it to be loud enough to hopefully be heard on the recording.

Paul responded cockily, "Don't really feel like talking."

"Answer the lady," Kyle ordered him. "I'm not afraid to use this gun and claim self-defense. Do what she said, and start talking."

"I came here to tell you who killed John."

I didn't miss the fact that Paul called his father by his name instead of calling him Dad. That had to mean something, right? Like he was distancing himself from what he did?

"Instead of telling the police?" I snorted in derision. "And you just brought your gun along for kicks? Try again."

Paul sighed dramatically. "I brought the gun in case nobody believed me and I needed to get away. I wasn't planning to actually use it."

"You couldn't call and tell Beckett that Donnie did it?" Marty asked. "Instead of breaking in here and lying in wait for her with a gun?"

"That was a questionable move," Jeff added, "breaking in here with three pickups parked out front. Did you really think you could sneak in with all of us here?"

"I saw you all leave together in that ridiculous yellow clown car," Paul explained, and I bristled at his description of my Pinto. "I thought you were just going to the DQ or something. I didn't know you'd be gone for hours."

"Explains the nap," Jeff mused.

"How do you know Donnie did it?" I asked.

He shouted back, "Had you not figured out he did it yet, Sherlock?"

"Want me to shoot him, Beckett?" Kyle asked. "Because I will."

I shook my head, even though he couldn't see me. "I don't

doubt it, but no. Paul, the police are already closing in on you. They know about you and Donnie working together. There's an eyewitness." There was no way he could know it was his sister, right? Not that it mattered now, since he'd soon be arrested for breaking into my house, if nothing else yet.

Paul scoffed. "No, there's not."

"Yep, there is," Marty said. "They saw you go in with your dad, then Donnie went in, then a little while later, Donnie came back out, and you came out a few minutes after him with blood on you. How would we know all that if somebody didn't see it? I know we'd all love to hear your explanation of what happened in *my* store." Nobody could've missed the emphasis on the "my."

"It's not supposed to be your store!" Paul shouted. "It was supposed to be mine! You should be in jail right now for John's murder, and I should be getting what's rightfully mine!"

The sound of sirens reached our ears, and Marty crossed the room to open the front door. I was afraid Paul wouldn't say any more before the police took him away.

"I'm telling you, it was Donnie!" Paul shouted. "I saw him do it. He killed John."

I shouted back, "That remains to be determined, but if that's true, why didn't you tell anyone this yesterday?"

"Because I was there, okay? Donnie could point the finger at me as easily as I could point it at him. I didn't want to be falsely accused of murdering my own father!"

Jeff responded, "But you were just fine and dandy with Marty being falsely accused of killing him?"

"Yes, because he didn't deserve the store! That's why we met John there."

"Hold on," I yelled. "How did you know Marty was going to inherit the store?"

"Donnie told me. This was all his idea. I was just the one who got John to the store."

"But why would you go along with it? You weren't going to inherit anything, with the new will in place."

"Donnie told me I was going to get half of John's money, even if I didn't get the store."

"Well, that wasn't true," Kyle stated unnecessarily.

"I know that *now*," Paul said with derision.

"So in essence," I said, "you killed your father for exactly zero reason other than to let some of his money get into Donnie's hands."

"No! For the twentieth time, I did not kill John! I'm not a killer!"

"Why did you need to bring a gun here if you're not a killer?" Kyle asked him.

Paul asked, "Why did *you* need to bring a gun here if *you're* not a killer?"

Kyle let out a sarcastic chuckle. "Because I'm protecting my friends from people like you, *Sherlock.*"

Chapter Twenty-Three

"Remember how I called the cops a few minutes ago?" Jeff asked.

"Duh," was Paul's response. He sounded like one of the teenagers at church.

"They told me they arrested Donnie," Jeff said, "and he said you planned to kill your dad all along—told him you were going to use a tool from the store and everything. He was just there to try to talk you out of it, but he was too late. I'm thinking the sentence for premeditated murder is going to be a lot worse than a spur-of-the-moment swing of an axe that might've been self-defense, if that's what *really* happened. I'm not inclined to believe Donnie's version."

Jeff was lying, because there was no way the police told him that, but I wasn't sure Paul knew that. I held my breath as I waited for Paul's response.

At that moment, Mitchell and Olivia raced into the house, guns drawn.

Paul immediately shouted, "I didn't do anything, officers! I'm just here minding my own business, and this guy is threatening to shoot me."

"You can put your gun down now, Kyle," Mitchell said as I crawled to the entrance into the kitchen so I could watch what was happening since Marty finally shifted his focus away from making sure I stayed out of sight.

Kyle placed his gun carefully on the kitchen counter and took several steps away from it. Mitchell and Olivia both had their guns trained on Paul.

"Your turn, Mr. Kemper," Mitchell ordered.

For a second, it seemed as if Paul might pull the trigger instead of relinquishing his gun, but he thankfully came to his senses and placed it on the table. Olivia leapt forward and confiscated it. Then she holstered her own weapon, but Mitchell kept his gun at the ready.

Mitchell asked, "Mr. Kemper, how'd you get in here, and why did you bring a gun?"

"Why aren't you asking why *he* brought a gun?" Paul jerked his head toward Kyle.

"I already know why he has a gun, and I'm talking to you at the moment. Answer my questions."

"I came in the back door," Paul stated. "And how do you know that's my gun? Maybe they forced me to put it in my hand before you got here so it would look like it was mine."

"He *broke* in the back door," I said. "You should be able to find evidence he picked the lock as well as his fingerprints on the door. And you won't find any of our fingerprints on that gun. He was waiting here for us when we got home, with the gun on the table next to him."

"All right, Mr. Kemper, you're under arrest for armed breaking and entering." Mitchell stalked to Paul and jerked him up out of his seat, and Olivia read him his rights as she cuffed him.

I said to Mitchell, "He told us he and Donnie cooked up this plan together, but Donnie is who actually killed John. I have no reason to believe Paul's not the killer, though. He's probably just trying to save his own skin."

"Hey!" Paul glared at me, but I ignored him. Then he turned his glare toward Mitchell. "I want a lawyer."

"I'm sure you do. I wouldn't suggest Donnie Masters."

Marty chuckled at Mitchell's response, and Paul sneered at him.

"We'll sort everything out down at the station," Mitchell replied. "And we'll see whose fingerprints match the ones on the letter and envelope." He gave Paul a not-exactly-gentle nudge toward the front door. "Let's go."

I rushed over to the stereo and ejected the tape.

"Hold on a sec." I held out the tape to Olivia. "I recorded our conversation. Hopefully it'll be helpful."

Paul cursed and glared at me yet again.

"Watch your mouth," Mitchell said as he escorted Paul out the door.

The rest of us watched as Mitchell and Olivia put Paul in the back of the squad car. Then Olivia got into the driver's seat, and Mitchell returned to the house with an evidence bag.

"I'm going to need you four to come down to the station to give your statements about this," he said as he put on one rubber glove and then placed Paul's gun in the bag, "and we'll also dust the back door for Paul's prints. Not tonight, though, because I'm sure we'll be with Paul for a while. Why don't you swing by the station in the morning? Even if we've made an arrest for the murder by then, we'll still want your statements for the trial."

"We can do that," I said. "And about that tape, I don't know if it caught everything Paul said, so here's what you need to know." I relayed what Paul revealed to us, with some help from the guys about what Paul was doing while we talked, since I couldn't see him.

"You also need to know what Jeff said to Paul right before you came in," I told Mitchell, "so you can maybe play along with it when you're questioning Paul."

I motioned for Jeff to repeat what he said to Paul, and he did.

"That could be helpful to get a confession," Mitchell said, "if he thinks he might be confessing to a lesser charge. Good work."

"Not my first rodeo with a murderer," Jeff said.

Mitchell cringed. "No, but I hope it's your last."

"Do you have any idea where Donnie is?" I asked Mitchell as he used his gloved hand to lock the back door.

"He's not home, but we'll find him," Mitchell assured us. "We've called in all the off-duty officers, since Jake and Frank won't be back from Springfield for another couple hours. I'll also ask the county sheriff's department to keep an eye out for him."

"You mentioned looking for fingerprints on the envelope," Marty said. "Does that mean they found it at John's house?"

"They did. It had John's name typed on the front. We'll check it for prints when they get back."

"Did they find the will?"

"Yes, and there's a discrepancy between the two. John's copy shows he left the VFW only 250 dollars. With that information and whatever Paul tells us, we can hopefully fill in some more gaps. The problem is going to be determining whether it was Paul or Donnie who swung the axe."

"Can you charge them both with murder," I asked, "even if you never know which of them did it?"

"It depends," Mitchell replied. "If we can prove they were both involved in the killing in some way, even if it's not clear which of them swung the axe, then yes. But it'll be better if we know."

"At least now we know for sure it wasn't Kathleen," I said. "We told Paul there was an eyewitness, and we detailed his, John's, and Donnie's movements. He didn't try to deny any of it, and he never mentioned his sister's name."

"Good to know," Mitchell replied. "I didn't think she was involved, but it's hard to be sure about these things without proof." He nodded toward Marty. "This means you're also fully off the hook now in the eyes of the law."

"Glad to hear it," my boyfriend replied.

Mitchell then looked each of the guys in the eye. "Don't leave Beckett alone until we have Donnie in custody, you hear me?"

They all readily agreed, and Mitchell headed out. As soon as the door closed, I threw my arms around Kyle and hugged him tightly.

"Thanks for saving our lives," I said.

He squeezed me back before letting me go. Marty immediately pulled me to him so my back was to his chest. He wrapped his arms around my shoulders and kissed the top of my head.

"I'm glad I was here," Kyle said. "And I'll be sleeping on your couch as long as Donnie's still running free out in the world." His gaze moved a few inches up so he was looking at Marty. "You're staying here, too, I'd imagine."

I felt Marty nod.

"Me, too, if you'll have me," Jeff added. "I can sleep on the floor as long as you've got an extra pillow."

"We've got three beds," I explained. "There's room for everyone."

Saying goodnight to Marty was a little different than the previous night. While the other guys used the showers, we relaxed against the headboard of the guest room bed, Marty's arm firmly curled around me.

He pressed his lips to my temple. "This all seems surreal."

"What does?" He could be talking about multiple things at this point.

"Everything. John being dead. Paul or Donnie killing him. You and me sitting in bed together."

I turned my head toward him and raised an eyebrow. "For the record, sitting is all we'll be doing in a bed until there's a gold band on both of our hands."

His lips twitched. "Wanna get married tomorrow?"

I playfully elbowed him in the side. "No, you silly man. I'm just making my wishes clear."

"And they'll be taken seriously," he said, searching my eyes. "I'll let you set the pace. I want you to be comfortable with anything we do."

I batted my lashes at him. "Well, I'm definitely comfortable with kissing."

He laughed and pulled me more tightly against his side. "I'm not sure kissing is a great idea when we're on a bed."

"I'll be good. I promise."

"Yeah, but I might not. I'll kiss you before you go back to your room, but not here in this bed."

I faked a pout and then lay my head against his shoulder. "You're no fun."

"Oh, we're going to have lots of fun together. Just you wait."

"Yeah?" I tilted my face so I could look at him. "What kinds of fun things are we going to do?" I gave him a stern look. "And I'm not talking about the bedroom kind of fun."

His laugh rumbled through me. "Okay, we'll talk about that kind of fun someday in the hopefully not-so-distant future. But for now, I think we should figure out a hobby we can do together."

"Really?" My nose scrunched up. "Like golf or fishing or bird-watching or something?"

He chuckled again. "If any of those things would make you happy, then yes. But I was thinking we both might enjoy something along the lines of woodworking, learning to play an instrument, something art related, or photography. Would any of those interest you?"

I smiled and nodded. "Yeah, I think I'd like to learn more about photography. I did photography in 4-H a few years when I was a kid, and I enjoyed it a lot. Cameras have really changed since then, though. I'd have to get new equipment." I looked at him again. "Unless you have a camera collection you've been hiding away somewhere?"

His cheeks pinked. "I've got a couple of decent cameras, and I set up a darkroom in my basement a few months ago."

"Really?" This was a side of Marty I didn't know about.

"Yeah, I like taking photos of wildlife and my land and even random stuff around my place." Marty lived on a few acres of farmland bordered by woods on the outskirts of town.

"Why didn't I know about this?" I pursed my lips and narrowed my eyes at him. "Does *anyone* know about this?"

He shrugged. "Kyle knows. I can't really hide it from him since he lives in my house and is nosy as all heck, as you well know. But I just do it for me. I don't enter photo contests and I'm not trying to sell my photos or submit them to magazines or anything."

"Maybe you should."

He ran his hand up and down my arm, sending tingles shooting through me.

"Maybe you should see my photos before you decide if they'd be good enough to win a contest or be in a magazine."

"All right. I want to see them tomorrow."

"Yeah?" He sounded wistful.

I sighed happily. "Yeah."

"What kind of photography do you think you'd like to do?" he asked.

"I think I'd like landscapes—all different kinds. And sunsets. I'm a big fan of sunsets."

"Then we'll travel around taking pictures of all kinds of land-scapes and sunsets."

A smile bloomed on my face, and I twisted sideways and slipped an arm behind Marty so I could wrap my arms around him and look up into his face. "You want to travel with me?" This was surprising, since one of the reasons things didn't work out with his ex-wife was because she wanted to travel a lot and he didn't.

"Of course I do." He brushed some hair out of my face and behind my ear. "If you want to travel, I'll be right there with you."

The edges of his mouth tilted down the slightest bit. "If you want me there, that is."

"Of course I do," I echoed his words. "I just thought that was one of the reasons you got divorced—because you don't like to travel."

He shook his head. "Travel was one of *many* reasons things didn't work out with her, but it's not that I didn't want to travel or that I don't like it. It's that I don't enjoy and, frankly, can't afford the kind of travel she wanted—jet-setting all over the world, staying at upscale resorts, eating at expensive restaurants while wearing fancy clothes. That's not me. And somehow I don't think it's you, either."

"It's not. I like to get all dressed up and go out on special occasions every now and then, but not all the time. And I'm all about road trips and staying in little roadside motels or even camping, as long as it's in a camper and not a tent. I like to see everything along the way to my destination, not fly over it."

"Road trips and camping are right up my alley. And I think I could handle taking you out for a fancy meal every now and then," he said with a smile, and a warm feeling spread through me at his words.

"I'd like that. I think I might want to try taking people pictures, too."

"People pictures, huh?" he teased. "You mean portraits? Like family photos, senior photos, that kind of thing?"

"Maybe. I don't know. I'd like to try a lot of different kinds of photography, if I'm honest. I'm glad you mentioned this idea. It really will be fun doing something like this with you."

"Yeah, it will."

We sat silently holding each other for a while, but it wasn't long before I felt myself drifting off. It had been a long day, and I wanted to get up early to head to the police station to give my statement about tonight and to see what the latest news was.

Marty whispered into my hair, "Let's get you to bed, sleepyhead."

He helped me up, but before he opened the door, he pulled me into his arms.

"Is it time for that kiss now?" I grinned up at him.

"Maybe more than one." He smirked. "If you're good."

I giggled. "I'm the best kisser you've ever known."

Then I tugged his mouth down to mine and proved it to him.

Chapter Twenty-Four

M arty, Kyle, Jeff, and I arrived at the police station at eight o'clock the next morning, after eating yet another meal fixed by Kyle. I told him he should consider opening a restaurant, and he scoffed, but then he looked like he actually might be considering the idea.

As it was Saturday, we didn't expect the police station's front door to be unlocked or to see Barbara at the front desk, but we were mistaken.

"We're here to give our statements about what happened at my house last night," I informed Barbara as the guys took seats in the small foyer, assuming we'd need to wait at least a few minutes. The door into the pit was closed, which was unusual.

Barbara gave me an assessing gaze. "You're not gonna ask what's happened since then?"

I shrugged. "I figured you wouldn't tell me, so there was no point in asking."

"Actually, I was just about to call you," she explained. "Detective Crowe asked me to do so if you hadn't shown up here by eight. He didn't want to bother you any earlier, in case you were sleeping in after all the events of last night."

"Yeah? What happened?" I asked eagerly. The men all leaned forward in their seats.

Barbara sat up straight, seemingly proud that she got to tell us this information. "A couple hours after Detective Crowe and Olivia arrived here with Paul, a county sheriff's deputy spotted Donnie's car out at his brother's place a few miles north of town. They let us know, and the guys went out there and brought him in."

We waited for her to continue the story, and when she didn't, I prompted her, "And then ... ?"

Barbara held her hands palm up. "That's all I can tell you."

I sighed in frustration. "Is Donnie at least still here? We don't need to worry about him coming after any of us?"

"He's been detained, is all I can say."

"Okay. Well, when can we give our statements?"

Barbara tapped her finger on a pile of clipboards on the corner of her desk. They all had blank papers clipped to them.

"You can write them down. That'll save time from them having to interview you one by one." She pointed her finger at each of us in turn. "And no talking to each other and comparing notes as you write. They need it all in your own words."

I handed out clipboards and pens to everyone, but before I began writing, I asked Barbara, "Can I at least talk to Mitchell? Or Frank?"

"We'll see."

She didn't budge from her desk or pick up the phone, so I asked, "How are they going to know I'm here?"

"They'll know if they come out here."

"You're not going to tell them?"

"Nope."

We settled in to write our statements, and about ten minutes later, the door into the pit opened, and Mitchell stepped into the foyer. His eyes lit up when he spied me, but his happiness was short-lived, making my heart hurt. He also had exhaustion written all over him.

I held up my clipboard. "We're writing our statements. We'd like to come back and talk to you, though, if you have a few minutes."

Mitchell's gaze swept the room, and for a second I thought he might deny my request, but then he relented. "All right. All of you can come back. I think you deserve that after last night and all your help with this case. But I can only give you five minutes."

That was good enough for me. I shot up out of my chair. "Let's go, boys."

Mitchell led us into the interview room, and the guys grabbed a couple extra chairs so we could all crowd around the heavy wooden table.

"I'll get straight to it," Mitchell said. "I guess Barbara told you we found Donnie."

"Yes, but that's all she said. Did he come without a fight?"

"Not exactly. When Frank and I went out to his brother's place with a couple of sheriff's deputies, he refused to come out. Without expressly saying it, he insinuated he had a gun, so we didn't try to force our way in. Then we called in everyone else from both forces who we could get in touch with, and once Donnie realized we weren't going away, he finally gave himself up."

"If he were smart, he would've come in without a fight," Kyle said. "He just made himself look guilty as heck."

"Exactly. When we got him back here, we told him there was a witness in the parking lot during the murder, and he admitted he was at the store that morning but that John was alive and perfectly healthy when he left. He said he didn't know John was going to be in town at all, and he simply followed him when he saw him leave Suzanne's house."

"That doesn't seem plausible," I said. "There's no way he could've seen John leave Suzanne's from his window and then have enough time to get to his car and out onto the street to be able to follow John before he was out of sight. And why would Donnie follow him anyway? That makes no sense."

"You're right. It doesn't," Mitchell said. "He's also claiming that it was John's copy of the will that was altered, but that makes no logical sense."

"So that's it, then?" Kyle asked. "We'll never know who actually did it?"

"We actually *do* know," Mitchell said with a smirk.

"What?" I exclaimed. "Why didn't you tell us that first thing?"

"I like to draw out the suspense," he replied.

I rolled my eyes. "Well, don't draw it out any longer!"

Mitchell nodded toward Jeff. "We played off what you said to Paul, and he sang like a parakeet. Claimed it was self-defense, but Donnie egged him on and then made sure John was dead. I think that last part is actually true. One detail we never told any of you is there were two partial footprints in the blood. One matched the boots Marty wore that day, but the other wasn't his. Without a warrant, we couldn't look for the other shoe before now. But we've matched it to a pair of Donnie's shoes, which still had small traces of blood on them, so we know he was there after John was killed."

Mitchell looked at me and then Marty. "Remember the button we found in the store? There was a partial print on it that matches Donnie. I doubt we'll ever find the clothes he was wearing, but at least the button not only puts him at the scene but implies he went upstairs and maybe into your office."

"So you've arrested both of them? They're in custody?" I asked, simply for reassurance.

"Yes. We're also looking through the VFW books and Donnie's bank accounts to see if he's been embezzling money." He tilted his head at me. "We got a tip that might be happening."

I grinned. "It was actually Edna's tip. I just passed it along."

"I'll make sure to give her credit for it. I can't see either of them getting bail," he added, "so you and Marty don't need to worry about your safety any longer."

"That's great to hear," Marty said.

"You've let Kathleen know?" I asked.

"Yes, I had just gotten off the phone with her when I went out and found you all in the foyer."

"Well," Kyle clapped his hands together once, "we wrapped this one up pretty quickly, huh?"

Mitchell chuckled and shook his head. "I guess we did. Thanks for your help—all of you."

"You'll make sure Olivia knows how much I helped?" Kyle asked eagerly.

Mitchell laughed again. "I'm pretty sure she knows. Though she probably wouldn't complain about you reminding her over dinner sometime."

"Excellent." Kyle rubbed his hands together in glee, and we all laughed.

"Guys," Mitchell said to Marty, Kyle, and Jeff, "would you mind giving me a minute with Beckett? You can finish your statements out in the foyer while you wait for her."

Jeff and Kyle quickly agreed and shook Mitchell's hand before heading out. Marty gave me a questioning look, and at my assenting nod, he also shook Mitchell's hand. The shake lasted longer than usual, with the two men having a silent conversation between them. Then they nodded at each other, and Marty slipped out of the room, closing the door behind him.

"Something interesting happened last night," Mitchell said.

"I'd say a lot of interesting things happened last night," I countered, and he chuckled.

"You're right, but this happened in between all the other interesting events, when I stopped to take a breath."

He looked down at his hands for a few moments, and I sat silently waiting for him to elaborate.

"After you told me we weren't going to be together," he looked back up into my eyes, "I was upset, yes, but I had this other feeling inside me. At first I wasn't sure what it was, but then I realized it was freedom. It was hope." He held up a hand in case I tried to interrupt. "Don't get me wrong. I didn't feel trapped with

187

you—not at all. But once a relationship with you was completely off the table, I realized I was free to truly acknowledge what I feel for Chris—what I've felt for her for a long time."

"Love," I said simply.

"Yeah, love. And not just she's-my-lifelong-best-friend kind of love. That's not to say I didn't love you. I did. I guess I still do, in a way. You'll always be special to me. But she's even more special, if you know what I mean."

I smiled softly at him. "I do know. You'll always be special to me, too. But …"

"Marty's even more special," he finished for me.

"Yeah."

"I think we're both going to end up with the perfect person for us. We wouldn't have been great together in the long run. I can acknowledge that now, even though I didn't want to for the past couple of months. I wouldn't have been happy living in Cherry Hill forever, and you wouldn't have been happy moving all over creation for my job. These last few days, I've seen how much you're an integral part of this town and how much you care about your friends and family, and vice versa. And I think whatever business you want to start, you're going to be successful, because you'll have the support of this entire community. They love you."

I placed my hand over my heart. "They love you, too. I hope you know that. You've done so much to help the people of this town get through a lot of heartache over the past year." Tears pricked behind my eyes.

"I'll always have a soft spot in my heart for Cherry Hill, there's no doubt about that."

I wiped a tear from my cheek. "I'm glad we're not parting on bad terms."

"Me, too. And I'm not just paying lip service when I say you've found a good man. As strange as it may sound coming from me, I'm glad about that. You deserve the love of a man who would do anything for you, and Marty would."

"You would've too," I said. "Don't sell yourself short."

"That's true. But I think this is all working out the way it was supposed to."

"I just hope Chris sees what she has in you and is willing to try again."

"Me, too, Beckett. Me, too."

Epilogue

Four Days Later

"I can't believe Darren and I missed an entire murder investigation while we were gone!" Aunt Star shook her head and then took a sip of her coffee.

"The investigation isn't over," I said from my spot across the table from her at The Check. "There's still a lot for them to figure out."

"You know what I mean."

"It's crazy how quickly everything happened," Trixie chimed in. "I knew about the murder, of course, but then I was blissfully unaware of the rest of it until my *best friend* finally remembered to call me Saturday morning, after the arrests were made." She gave me a mock glare, and I patted her arm.

The three of us, plus my mom, Veronica, and Suzanne were seated at two tables shoved together in the back of the diner. I'd gotten up before the crack of dawn yet again to meet the ladies for breakfast before everyone needed to go to work. I was sure I'd see them all again that evening at John's funeral visitation, but that wouldn't be the best place to have this conversation.

Aunt Star and Darren returned home from their cruise late the night before, and they both stayed at his house as planned, so they wouldn't bother me when they came home. But the second they heard the news about the murder when they arrived home and checked the messages on Darren's answering machine, my aunt called me. Instead of explaining every detail over the phone, I gave her the highlights and then invited her to breakfast with Trixie and me, which then led to inviting the other ladies as well. Suzanne had also returned to town the prior evening after her aunt's funeral, so none of us had seen her yet since the murder.

Veronica said, "I can't believe I wasn't there for the excitement Friday night!"

"Be glad you weren't," I said. "Not that I wouldn't have appreciated your help or your company, but having a gun pointed in your vicinity is no fun. I don't recommend it."

"At least you weren't alone," Veronica said. "I'm glad the guys were there with you for all of it."

"Me, too."

"Suzanne," my mom said, "I'm so sorry about John. He was a good man."

Suzanne nodded and wiped her eyes. "He was. Thank you. And I'm sorry I didn't tell anyone we'd been seeing each other. I just didn't want to be the focus of town gossip. You know how it can be."

The rest of us nodded politely, well aware she was typically the stream powering Cherry Hill's gossip mill.

I cleared my throat. "Somehow the grapevine hasn't managed to pick up on another piece of juicy gossip."

Mom, Trixie, and Veronica knew what I was about to share, but the others didn't. They looked at me expectantly when I paused for effect after my statement.

I continued, "Marty and I are officially dating."

Aunt Star gave me a knowing smile. I think she knew all along who I was going to choose.

Suzanne pressed her hands over her heart. "I was hoping you'd come to your senses and snap that man up." She nodded and tears filled her eyes again. "I'm so glad John left the store to him. He deserves it."

"He does," I said. "And I'm going to start helping out some at the store behind the scenes—doing the bookwork and some advertising and things like that."

"You'll be good at that," Mom said, much to my surprise. "You were made for bigger things than being the church secretary." She glanced at Veronica. "No offense."

Veronica shrugged. "None taken. I agree that Beckett should be doing more than what she's allowed to do at church. Those deacons have too much power."

"There's nothing wrong with being a secretary," I said, "and I don't plan to leave that job at the moment. But you're right. I feel like I could do so much more if only I had more freedom, and working with Marty part-time will give me that. The two of us are also going to explore photography a little bit in our spare time. I'm hoping that might turn into something more, too."

"Ooo, we need a photographer based here in Cherry Hill," Suzanne said. "I've always hated having to go over to Taylorville to get family pictures taken."

"You always took great shots when we were in 4-H, and you got a couple of gold ribbons at the fair," Trixie mused. "Add that to you being a people person, and I think you'd be great at being a professional photographer, if it's something you decide to do."

I smiled at my friend. "Thanks, Trix."

"Did Cynthia make it home safely?" Veronica asked my mom.

"Cynthia?" Aunt Star said, looking at Mom and then me. "Was she here?"

I filled her in on what brought her other niece to Cherry Hill.

"Yes," Mom finally answered Veronica, "her parents drove

through here Sunday afternoon on their way home from Peoria. They didn't want her driving back to Arkansas alone."

"She might be back this summer, though," I informed Aunt Star. "Edna let her help write the article about the murder for the newspaper before she left. She told Cynthia if she'll come back this summer for a month or so, she'll give her a job and let her see if she enjoys journalism as much as she thinks she will."

"I hope you told her she could stay with us," Aunt Star said.

"I did, and Mom also offered her my old room. I guess you two are going to have to fight over her. Just keep it civil," I teased.

I caused some tension between my mom and her sister when I moved back to Cherry Hill and decided I'd have more freedom if I lived with my aunt instead of my parents. Mom finally got over it, but it took a while. The two were now closer than they'd ever been, though, so I knew they'd be okay with whatever Cynthia chose to do.

"Wherever she decides to stay is fine with me," Mom said. "It would just be great to spend some time with her before she goes off to college in the fall. Who knows how much we'll get to see her after that. She'll be off who knows where living her life, and we'll only see her once a year, if that."

"Back to you and Marty," Suzanne said to me, "I guess it's pretty serious if you're going to be working with him. Are there wedding bells in the future?"

I couldn't stop the smile that bloomed on my face at the thought of being Mrs. Marty James someday. "We just started dating, Suzanne. Let's not get ahead of ourselves."

"You know I love Marty," Mom said, "but I don't want you to rush into anything. There's no reason not to take your time and be absolutely certain he's the one before you walk down the aisle."

I was a little surprised by my mom's statement, since she was often hinting about wanting more grandkids and she knew that wouldn't happen until I was married.

"I'll be smart about it, Mom," I assured her. "You don't have to worry about us running off to Vegas or anything."

"Good." She nodded decidedly.

"Speaking of running off," Trixie said, "I want to hear all about the cruise, Starla. Scott and I have talked about going on one as a tenth anniversary trip."

I began singing the theme song to *The Love Boat*, and everyone laughed.

As my aunt regaled the table with stories from her trip, I sat back and enjoyed being in the presence of so many people I loved. Like Mitchell had pointed out, these were my people. I had carved out a spot for myself—a life for myself—here in Cherry Hill, and I couldn't imagine being anywhere else.

The bell over the diner's door jingled, and I glanced that way to see a man striding toward me with a single-minded focus—not just any man, but *my* man. The entire table fell silent as he approached, but he didn't acknowledge the other women's attention. Instead, he leaned down and gave me a not-quite-chaste kiss on the lips. Then he grabbed an empty chair from a nearby table and slotted it into the space we made for him between Trixie and me.

"Morning, ladies," Marty said as he slung an arm across the back of my chair. "Carry on with whatever you were talking about. I'm just here because I can't seem to stay away from this one. Hope that's okay."

He pressed a kiss to my temple to a chorus of "awww's" from the rest of the women.

I gave him a soft smile. "You're always welcome at my table."

Have you read the first four Totally 80s Mysteries?

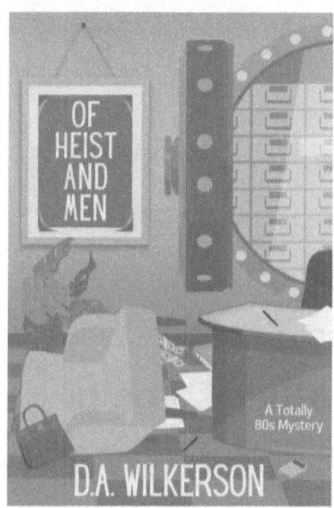

Available at Amazon.com

Throwback RomComs

Author Dana Wilkerson also writes romcoms set in Chicago in the late 1980s! These books are loosely connected to the Totally 80s Mysteries and feature some of Beckett's cousins and their friends.

Available at Amazon.com

Mystery Journals

Do you want an easy way to keep track of all the suspects or other characters in mysteries? These journals allow mystery readers to record suspects, other characters, motives, means, opportunity, and more!

Available at Amazon.com

If you enjoyed this book, join author D.A. Wilkerson's mailing list!

When you join the list, you don't just receive a few emails a month. You get book and music playlist recommendations, 1980s nostalgia, writing updates, sneak peeks of upcoming books, subscriber-only freebies and discounts, and more. Come join the fun!

To join, go to danawilkerson.com and click "Sign Up."

About the Author

D.A. (Dana) Wilkerson is the author of the Totally 80s Mysteries cozy mystery series and the Throwback Romcoms series (as Dana Wilkerson). She has been a professional writer and editor for almost two decades and was the collaborative writer of two non-fiction *New York Times* best sellers: *The Vow: The True Events That Inspired the Movie* (Kim and Krickitt Carpenter) and *Balancing It All* (Candace Cameron Bure).

Dana lives in Oklahoma and enjoys traveling, reading, being an aunt, binge-watching crime shows, and attending Oklahoma City Thunder basketball games.

danawilkerson.com